MW01632878

The Arc and the Sediment

The Arc and the Sediment

Christine Allen-Yazzie

Christine Allen-Yazzie

Utah State University Press
Logan, Utah

Utah State University Press
Logan, Utah 84322-7800
www.usu.edu/usupress/

Manufactured in the United States of America
Printed on acid-free paper

***

Library of Congress Cataloging-in-Publication Data

Allen-Yazzie, Christine Diane.
The arc and the sediment / Christine Allen-Yazzie.
p. cm.
ISBN 978-0-87421-654-7 (acid-free paper)
1. Women alcoholics--Fiction. 2. Women authors--Fiction. 3. Interracial marriage--Fiction. 4. Separated people--Fiction. 5. Navajo Indians--Fiction 6. Voyages and travels--Fiction. 7. Deserts--Fiction. I. Title.
PS3601.L439A73 2007
813'.54--dc22

2007004631

"Nature abhors a vacuum."

—Empedocles

"Nothing exists but atoms and the void."

—Democritus

"…just as heavy bodies, when rising, move more rapidly in the lower region where the propelling force is, and more slowly in the higher; and when the force which originally propelled them no longer acts upon them, they return to their natural position, that is, to the surface of the earth."

—Hero of Alexandria, "Treatise of Pneumatics," 100 A.D.

Table of Contents

The Plan

Tonight Gretta will arrive sometime about midnight in Fort Defiance, Arizona, to retrieve her husband in time for their ninth anniversary. Failing that, she'll deliver to him his eagle-bone whistle. A three-legged Chihuahua will announce her arrival. Her little feet and broad shoulders will be admitted into a tidy if dilapidated single-wide where she is not especially welcome. If all goes as planned, Lance will follow her out of the trailer house and down the splintering stairs, and step into their pickup. The two of them will stop at a motel just outside the reservation, look at each other like shame-faced dogs from either side of a well-worn queen-sized bed. It's possible they'll have makeup sex. Gretta has shaved her legs, just in case. In the morning, they will go home to their two children, who might or might not be sitting up in their beds. Together, they will deliver news of either a reunion or a divorce. Together, they will work out the details.

Or that was Gretta's thinking at about seven o'clock this morning.

The Plan, Amended

THERE IS something beautiful about a golden naked woman lying in the sand, which is why Gretta is stretched out here in the not-terribly-hot late-afternoon sun. But she is not a golden naked woman looking beautiful in the sand. Her face is swollen from drinking gin and is blazing vermilion like the redrock around her. Her sunglasses pressure her temples and the pajamas wadded up beside her smell like the janitorial closet of an old, canasta-addicted smoker. Her hair is tangled and salty, her doughy belly an aurora borealis of two long, nearly unendurable pregnancies. Peering through the window between lens and cheekbone, she sees that she is shaped like a crevice, like a V, and at the bottom of the V is hatred lying fallow, which is not, by definition, beautiful.

In the front pocket of her army-surplus pack is the whistle, wrapped in an orange-and-white bandana. She takes it out, uncovers it to see that it's still real, and looks at it without touching. She removes her sunglasses. Not a glimmer. The whistle, broken in two pieces, is dry and inanimate. What once braced the weightless wing of an enormous bird of prey now clacks top end against bottom, protected only by a bandana from her trembling hand.

She doesn't know why Lance trusted her with the thing. It was given to him in an event that involved days of praying, fasting, and sweating for reasons presumably too great, too indescribable, too *Indian* to share with her. Maybe this oddly placed trust is why she hopes to make amends with her husband. Maybe it's why she doesn't trust him.

Pneumatic. Is it a word?

She'll be glad to be rid of the thing, of the responsibility of it, but as yet, she still hasn't thought of something appropriate to say to Lance, and the detour she hoped would inspire the words is, rather, making her sleepy. She wraps the whistle back up and tucks it into the front pocket of her pack. She fumbles around the main cavity—four books, a few tampons, a stack of credit cards (both good and bust), a driver's license (technically invalid, given that her neurologist refuses to declare her seizure-free at this time), receipts, more receipts, a bra, cigarette butts (stinking up everything—she smells her fingers—*Jesus*), a dictionary, a beat-up flip phone.

No reception. She climbs an outcropping of rock. She slips, scrapes a knee and an elbow, bleeds, but finds herself oddly in range.

A lizard skitters close, assesses her with pushups. She takes a photo of it with the phone. Her daughter might forgive her if she brought home such a thing, worthy of any second-grade show-and-tell—such delicate hands, a blush of blue spreading from underbelly to soft pulsing throat, curious half-closed eyelids. She could keep it in something for now—*the console? the glove box?*—then buy a cage in Moab.

Gretta lunges. She is rewarded with a discarded tail.

Ice cream it is, she thinks. It's just as well—the Navajo in her daughter isn't supposed to handle reptiles. Of course, now that Lance has left her, Gretta may have to reconsider the zodiac of cultural prohibitions they sutured together between the two of them and settle on which ones remain pertinent. If he doesn't return, he will be responsible for seeing through his own.

"Thank you for calling Moab's own Golden Granary Pharmacy, where customers always come first. Para Español, marqué uno. To order refills by phone, press two now…"

It's not like her meds will work with as much as she's been drinking anyway. A voracious bender presented itself some five days ago and will end, in all likelihood, this afternoon—hopefully at a Laundromat. Once Lance is in-hand, or clearly not, she'll get her Dilantin. At least she has Zoloft. *Just breathe. Just breathe now.*

Pneumatic. This is how it is: A word drifts from the ether into her nostrils, her ears, permeates the membranes of her eyes, and she must look it up, given the limited pool of language a Utah railroader upbringing and four and a half years of state college have afforded her.

Pneumatic—pneumonia? "Moved or worked by..."

She sets her dictionary down and weaves across and around patches of cryptobiotic soil to the truck, heckling herself—she drove a couple of miles off the off-road, after all, probably over yards and yards of the fragile stuff, and now she tiptoes. One day, she will be an environmentalist in more than just theory. Maybe she'll even be a vegetarian, except that she will eat fish, because fish, she is willing to believe, are too stupid to contemplate their own demise.

She will be a woman whose socks match. When they get holes in the heels, she will throw them away and buy new socks—thick, soft knee-highs, not the junk socks she buys at Wal-Mart. *Hell,* she thinks, *you won't step foot in a Wal-Mart.* Instead, she'll pontificate on the moral depravity of superstores.

One day she will teach her kids Tulip and Braden to eat bran cereal rather than Cap'n Crunch. She will eat bran cereal, or at least she will make bran muffins. She will lock her doors at night. She will expect her children to brush their teeth not once, but twice a day. She will brush her teeth twice a day. She will wash her hands rigorously after every pee.

And if she is divorced, she will make serious efforts to use the term *Native American* instead of *Indian.* Unless, of course, her children bristle at her use of the words as her in-laws always seem to have, in which case she will be all appeasement.

One day she will be sober—for good. For now, she yanks her laptop's power cord out of the inverter and returns with laptop and pack to the outcropping. She makes an office of a pocket of sand. The laptop burns her thighs as she types, heated by sun and inverter both.

WordsforLater.doc

Pneumatic: Moved or worked by air pressure. Adopted for holding or inflated with compressed air. Having air-filled cavities. Of or relating to the pneuma:

spiritual. Having a well-proportioned feminine figure; esp., having a full bust.

The whistle is Lance's pneumatic Leatherman, his tool of potentiality. It opens, it sharpens, it seals, it heals. But it's selective. It allows only good intentions to pass through it. Lance rarely uses it, but the possibility awaits him like an obedient dog.

Gretta wants a tool. She has a laptop and a dictionary, and they serve her well, but are not of the spiritual variety—any positive renderings are arguably incidental. The idea behind the whistle is that it can make everything right, or at the very least say thanks, because that's what it was meant to do. She considers whether she is capable of saying thanks—wholeheartedly, with feeling.

WordsforLater.doc

Occident: To fall, to set.

Occidental: Of, relating to, or situated in the Occident: western. A member of the Occidental peoples: a person of European ancestry.

Occlude: Obstruct; to come together with opposing surfaces in contact; used of teeth.

Of teeth? As in the sand grit grinding around between my molars? Here's proof that the laptop and the dictionary don't make everything right. Instead, the cursor and the word reveal the world to be frightening and inconclusive, and they give form to just anything—murder, desire, self-defeat, love. Infidelity.

She imagines James, Lance's brother, standing on the deck of the *USS Reagan*, shielding his eyes from an unrelenting sun to watch inky black clouds billow into the sky from the oil fields of a foreign shore.

She sets the laptop aside, lies on her back, covers her eyes with an arm. With or without words—or, for that matter, blue-bellied lizards—the world is a gaseous place.

"...To leave a message with a pharmaceutical representative, press three now. To contact the grocery or the Super Saver Photo Lab, press four now. To learn more abut our Golden Granary Customer Rewards program, press five now. To hear pharmacy hours…"

> ***WordsforLater.doc***
>
> **Gaseous:** Having the form of or being gas; also: of or relating to gases. Lacking substance or solidity; GASSY <trick phrases and *gaseous* circumlocutions —Edwin Newman>

Sand wafts into her nose and mouth, tasting of chalk. She rolls over for a bug's-eye view. She sees just what's in front of her but understands there are miles and miles of the stuff: in the beds of canyons, at the bases of buttes, in the crevice of her ass and the holes of her ears. In a photo the banks of sand might look like you could spray them with whipped cream and take a slice, but up close, there's nothing pure about them. Ants and spiders and snakes make trails, traversing sticks and stickers without notice, tracing Ss in the sand. When she breathes in, her cheek pressed against the warmth, the granules rub at an already sore throat. When she breathes out, dust drifts into her eyes. Her hipbones sink into the sand and her back arches till it aches.

She checks her voice-mail. Lance's mother Renee has left four messages on her answering machine, telling her to stay away, Lance has a new life she need not interfere with. "You leave that boy alone. He's getting a new life. He's got his way, and you got yours." Gretta wonders whether Renee sees their children as part of Lance's old life or his new one. She would like to know when he crossed the line between then and now. To Gretta, it is one life—her life—and the lines are made up of prejudice and accident, not time.

She replays two saved messages from her own mother. "Did you register the Hoover yet? You have to register the damned thing if you expect them to honor the warranty. I didn't buy you a vacuum just so you could break it and not have it fixed. God knows you'll break it eventually." She can't deny it—she's a breaker of small appliances. Or at least, an abandoner. Her last vacuum was used, her grandmother's.

She couldn't figure out how to remove the bag, much less find one the right size to replace it. The sales rep at Sears laughed at her. "Wow… this old thing? I don't know…." The bag ultimately became so full of sediment, it exploded and she itched for two days. Rather than admit she didn't have the will to e-bay for antique vacuum bags, she told her mother the thing's motor died a sad death in an incident involving yarn and tacks.

"To delete, press seven…."

Her mother's second message: "Gretta? Is that you? Look, honey, there's something wrong with your voice-mail. I'm just hearing noises and a beep. Are you there? Is this a trick? I'm concerned."

Gretta finishes off a pint of Gilbey's gin and fills it with red sand—a bottle of magic sand, she tells herself—a tool with which she can appropriate herself to an ideal life: motherhood, gainful employment, bay windows, unexpected pleasant circumstances.

Her husband is unclear to her now. She wonders whether she has ever seen him in a moment of clarity. The memory of his face seems overexposed in the harsh afternoon light, a fleshy russet potato of a map. She sees not his parting words, but the words she has used to describe his face: wide, elegant, thick-lipped, summoning, dividing. At times, an undershot jaw. She has been told the dark lips trace the health of liver, of heart. She sees also the words with which he has been described to her: an angry brow, accusatory eyes, a willful stride, a knowing grin.

"What, he wants his land back?" her uncle said once, studying a framed photo Gretta had hung in the hallway—an image of a Red Cloud quote scrawled on the wall of a BIA office during an AIM siege: "'They made us many promises, more than I can remember, but they never kept but one, they promised to take our land, and they took it.'" He shook his head with the force of certain cartoon characters, said, "It ain't never going to happen. They might as well get used to it. Why they always have to walk around so pissed off all the time is beyond me. It's not like we call them savages or shoot them off a horse anymore." He pointed to a black-and-white Gretta had taken of Lance at L.A.'s Venice Beach, at sunset. "See there? Pissed off. Got an attitude. If I didn't know him personally, I'd say he was a cup-half-empty kind of guy."

WordsforLater.doc

Savage: A person belonging to a primitive society; a brutal person; a rude or unmannerly person, at least in some cultures.

Saveloy: Pig's brains; a ready-cooked, highly seasoned dry sausage.

At one time, Gretta too might have seen him as saveloy do, but now he is just Lance, willing himself to smile for the camera despite the sun setting in his eyes. His is the face she has woken to thousands of mornings—sometimes pleasant, sometimes irritated, usually just reluctant to turn off the alarm and get out of bed. *No,* she reminds herself—now he is not even that familiar face, but an ambiguity pressing against her lower regions, a force that will not have her.

A fire ant chases aimlessly across her thigh; she flicks it off. She's certain she'd be hungry if she didn't have the spins and a massive headache. She sits up, brushes the sand off her arms, checks herself over for ants and other trespassers. When she reaches for her clothes, the alcohol in her blood whirls into motion, flooding her extremities all at once, making her blood flow a fine, decorative pink. She lies back down to catch her breath, steady her vision, but her eyes report a world lacking in vertical indices. The sand consumes her warmly.

New Breasts = New Bras

GRETTA WAKES to sunburned skin, chilled flesh. The laptop is hibernating. The dictionary is stretched open; she puts it back in her pack. She stands up too quickly, waits for the blackness to subside. Finally she is hungry—fiercely hungry, fourth-month hungry if she were pregnant, which, thank god, she is not.

She will finish her work, which will travel from brain cell to keyboard to hard drive to cell phone to satellite to her boss's wireless-equipped gray-taupe cubicle, not excessively beyond her deadline. Not long after that she will find her way back to civilization, back to food, and deliver the eagle-bone whistle to Lance. The thing, after all, is rightfully his. She wants to show him that she knows it; she wants to acknowledge its importance. She wants also to release herself of it and leave in his hands its brokenness. But first, she will get dressed, then.... *Then.*

Then she will work some more. Maybe even take something up on the side—waitress again, if she has to.

UtahCitizen.doc

The impervious brassiere, that modern-day successor to yesteryear's corset, was patented in November 1914 by New York debutante Mary Phelps "Polly" Jacob. The elastic "freedom fighter," as it has been called by some, was fashioned in haste, and with the assistance of the lady's French maid Marie and her needle, out of two silk pocket handkerchiefs, pink ribbon, and thread. The women couldn't have known that the prototype bra, designed to flatten the bust against the chest, would come to represent the very antithesis of women's pneumatic fight for freedom.

Despite riots and bra burnings taking place at campuses across the nation, the *Dilbert* financial page has posted a recommendation to buy Maidenform. "Why?" the stock analysts ask. "Because breast implants are up 40% in the last two years. New breasts=new bras."

To Food

"YOU GOING to pay for that?" a woman asks. She's wearing a park ranger hat and a stiff green T-shirt.

Gretta apologizes profusely. Holding an open bag of corn nuts in one hand and an empty bag of M&Ms in the other, she insists she was about to pay. "I'm just so hungry," she explains with food in her mouth, nodding toward a long and growing line at the cash register.

Another woman peeks over the display.

"You have white stuff...." Park Ranger waves as a lap swimmer might toward one corner of her mouth.

"Powdered donuts." Gretta swallows too much too fast, winces, wipes her mouth with the back of her hand. "I'll pay for them too. The package is...in my pocket. Until I pay."

The other woman walks around the aisle. "Do you like my sister's shirt?" Park Ranger asks.

"Yeah. Curious George is all right...I guess," Gretta says. "Look, I have money—"

"Come on," Curious George says to Park Ranger, laughing. "I don't need your help."

"Where you heading?" Park Ranger asks, studying Gretta's sandals. Gretta sees then that Smokey the Bear, embroidered on the brim of the green hat, is smoking weed. She realizes the woman is not, after all, a park ranger.

"Me? Nowhere," Gretta says.

"Seriously. You live here? You traveling?" Her arms and shoulders are thin but soft and she totters as she talks.

"South. I'm going south."

"My sister and I were just looking for a place to hike. Know any good places?"

"Let's go," Curious George says, annoyed now. The two look alike, mostly. Curious has a smaller chin, compelling eyes, unruly eyebrows.

"Yeah. I just…well, I just saw a place. I was just there. Not far from here."

"You wouldn't want to show us, would you?"

"Karen! Let's go."

"We packed a lunch—turkey sandwiches. Ham sandwiches if you don't like turkey. Avocados. Strawberries."

Curious George giggles in spite of her urgings.

"Raspberries and cream. Corona. Some healthy shit too, if that's your thing—dried-up exotic peas and sad little apricot ears and god knows what else. Nasty shit. Bincy's shit."

"Bincy?"

"As in 'Itsy Bitsy Spider.' That was her favorite song. But she always said *incy bincy*. You know…." She does the spider with her hands.

Gretta knows. A longing for her kids belts her in the back.

Bincy slugs her sister. "I'm going," she mouths. Then, to Gretta, "Sorry about my sister."

"No, it's okay. I just thought for a second there…I guess I thought she was going to arrest me or something."

"She's always trying to hook me up with someone. Last rest area, it was a Dish sales rep. She thinks I'll fuck, like, whoever."

"Thanks."

"I mean, not that you're *whoever*. But you know—I don't know you."

"Lot of good it does," Karen says. She excuses herself to the restroom.

"She thought she had you figured, with your necklace and all." Bincy sizes her up as she talks but seems confused. "Where'd you get it?"

“This? Yeah, my first girlfriend gave me this—like, over a decade ago.” Gretta looks at the pendant, a silver lambda on an onyx triangle, as if for the first time. “So I mean, maybe your sister wasn’t entirely off-radar.” She smiles as best she can, wonders if she still has powder on her face.

“And…she’s not entirely on, is she?”

Gretta shrugs. The need to drive south wanes. Bincy, Gretta sees, has freckles. Tiny near-transparent freckles that oppose the look of worry and impatience she wears. She would like to learn more about the freckles.

“Follow me,” Gretta could say. Or, “I’m likely getting a divorce.” Instead, she thinks of the magic of her bottle of sand, or lack thereof, and finds that she isn’t ready for it to work or fail to work on her marriage. She is on the road still, seeing what she can see. She puts the CornNuts bag and the donuts and the M&Ms bag on a display and fumbles through her pack. “Here—I’ll draw you a map.” She uses a checkbook deposit slip to draw the map.

“This is where you live?” Bincy points to the address and phone number on the deposit slip.

“Yeah.”

“Lance and Gretchen Bitsilly—”

“Gretta—that’s…call me Gretta.”

“Who’s Lance?”

Concentrate: West of the highway. Then what? What were the markers? “The uh…water spout. I mean, he was.”

“Was?”

Now that Gretta’s drawing a map, she feels unsure of how she got to her spot—or, for that matter, back here, to a Sinclair. “That’s cool, you’re on a trip with your sister,” she says when she finishes, or more accurately gives up. “Wish I had a sister who’d go on road trips with me.” She is unnerved by the way Bincy looks at her, by the tugging sense that she she should offer some disclaimer regarding Lance.

“You’re red,” Bincy says.

“I’m sunburned.”

"Sorry. That came out wrong." She mock-smiles, as an irritated flight attendant might, and as quickly loses the smile. She takes a business card out of her fanny pack. "I don't work at the clinic anymore, but my cell number's on the back." JANICE TUELLER, LCSW. Gretta sees she also lives in Salt Lake, or worked there, at one time.

"Call me. I mean, if the spout runs dry. Or not. Maybe you can come with me and Karen sometime, hang out. We go hiking a lot. We don't hike so much. Mostly we just hang out."

"That's my kind of hiking." Gretta fumbles for her keys, wonders just how long it would take for a licensed clinical social worker to realize she is more baggage than she is worth. "And—damn, where'd I put them?—you have my number too. Don't forget." She pushes the exit door open with her back; a bell chimes.

"Hey Gretta," Bincy (*Janice!*) says.

"Yeah?"

"Don't forget to pay. For your food, I mean."

Dear James

SOMETHING GRETTA read last night bothers her, and it will not wait another mile. She's back on the highway, some twenty miles past the Sinclair. She parks on the shoulder with engine running and returns to her laptop. She pushes *M. Butterfly* open and braces it with the lip of the laptop.

```
M.Butterfly.doc

Dancers help him put on the Butterfly wig.

GALLIMARD: I have a vision. Of the Orient. That, deep
within its almond eyes, there are still women. Women
willing to sacrifice themselves for the love of a man.
Even a man whose love is completely without worth.
```

Still, it is not enough. It is not enough to read, not enough to copy it down. Still she is bothered. And it probably has little to do with the opera *Madame Butterfly*, which she was assigned to review in February, or her copy of the play *M. Butterfly*, which she glommed on to in order to justify her resentment toward the production. It is something else, something buried in—maybe the same thing that compels her to pack the book around with her at all times, a Magic 8 Ball she cannot do without, just like the handful of other books she carries with her.

Her jaw aches with nervousness and her fingers necessarily come to rest on the keyboard. She couldn't begin to paraphrase along her own lines to get a feel for the mess of it all because she is not yet sure whether to cast herself as soldier or Butterfly. Surely she has never sacrificed for the love of a man. *Even a man whose love is completely without worth.* Who would? Why give in? Nor would she sacrifice for the love of a woman. In a state like Utah.... She could sacrifice *for* her children, but she wouldn't sacrifice her children *to* a homophobic state with a completely out-of-control DCFS struggling to cover its payroll—not for love, not for anything. *So why—*

And concubine? Butterfly was not a role she wanted to fill for any amount of money. Yet if anyone were a concubine in her marriage, it wouldn't be Lance. She couldn't see him as soldier either.

James, then?

Not a soldier, but a sailor. *Lance's brother...shit.*

She gives up for lack of entry. Anyway, her fingers muddle her thinking with their aching—when they are not grasping the wheel, they are clenched in fists or typing like mad or clutching a drink. She stretches them, presses against each palm between thumb and fingers, and still they ache.

Sacrifice—*blood of, for your country, all the little lambs.* She taps palm to forehead. Should she? Might she have? *For the love of whom?* For the love of a man. For the love of a woman. For the greater good. For Great Expectations. For God's sake.

Perhaps it is James—or Gretta's extensive correspondence with him—that she should sacrifice. Or perhaps it is only James among them who will ever (to use the language of CNN, Fox, and MSNBC pundits) "know sacrifice." The next-to-ultimate sacrifice: surviving war. Or one step up: becoming a white wooden statement in the Camp Casey outdoor armoire.

For the love of his country. For the love of a country offering rotating, bottom-of-the-screen, up-to-the-minute headlines regarding celebrity spats, age-prevention technology, and military obits. For the love of a country who'd rather watch a black man drown than send him a bus to flee a flood. Add to that a suite of ever-diminishing veteran health benefits—reductions of hospital beds in veteran hospitals, limits on prosthetics available for the mutilated, increased copays and deductibles for returned soldiers and their families.

For the love of—

For the love of a country offering ungrateful, unpatriotic, unheroic me.

Of course, James's choice to join the navy couldn't have had anything to do with being stuck in a warehouse job in Idaho with no marketable outside skills. Nor did it have anything to do with being turned away by the Navajo Nation for scholarship money, as he had no friend or relative working within the fluorescent-lit walls of the frustratingly despondent and nepotistic tribal scholarship office: "…we did not receive your application…," "…we did not receive your application…," "…we did not receive your application…," "…we did not receive your application…," "…we did not receive your application.…"

Dancers help him put on the Butterfly wig. Dancers help him put on the Butterfly wig. Dancers help him—

DearJames.doc

Dear Cricket,

I'm finally traipsing off to Arizona to see what your big brother is up to. I'm on that big stretch of highway in Utah that you always called The Sleeper.

The desert is not so hot after all: seventy-something degrees. It's supposed to warm up tomorrow. A late summer, I'm told. Just missed a bout of rain, I'm told. I'll bet it's hotter than hell in your neck of the woods.

Having all kinds of problems with the Chev—overheats, engine doesn't want to turn over, makes a hideous sound arbitrarily, windows get stuck, one wiper's broken. Your mother hates me more than probably ever.

Heard about all those kidnappings last week. I guess you're safe onboard, yes? Tell me more about the lights at night. Who is burning the oil, us or them?

Haven't got a letter from you in weeks, but if you were dead, I assume someone would tell me. Wouldn't they?

Yes, I know about the bananas. Very talented women, I've heard. Next time you're on leave, send me a souvenir. Something involving silk or stone. Not bananas.

Listen, I know they said you're fine, safe, whatever. I'm just saying if you start twitching or something—I mean, if your vision gets blurry and you get swelling and headaches and stuff—tell someone. Outside of the military. Hasn't the gov't done enough to fuck up your family? Fish and Game steals all your mom's and dad's feathers, and you what? Want to defend their country? Why don't you ask the southern tribes down by New Orleans whether their country loves them enough to fish them out of a flood. Oh, you can't! They were washed away. Guess FEMA wasn't aware they existed so they didn't send help.

I'm not saying I'm not proud of you. I just want you safe. Take it from a woman whose advice isn't entirely without worth. I was right about the insurance, wasn't I? I was right about the pianist. Sometimes I know some things.

Thanks for letting me send you off properly. It was a great trip. I miss you too—missed you even before you left. When we celebrate your return, there'll be no tequila, I promise. I don't even like tequila. Surprise. Hey, let's go to D.C. sometime when I'm out there. But I must say, it's getting harder and harder to find baby-sitting—and excuses. The kids might have to come visit Uncle James.

Your nephew is, just so you know, fully potty-trained. Thank you, Reece's Pieces.

Love,

G.

You Got to Cut Its Throat

EITHER GRETTA will arrive in Arizona and ask for Lance's return or she will announce her need for a divorce.

Either Lance will be living at his aunt's trailer house or she will find him living with someone else.

If he is at Aunt Angela's, he will either agree or disagree with her request, whatever it be.

Either Lance will change his mind or he will not.

Either Gretta will change her mind or she will not.

Either she will arrive stinking of gin or she will refrain. Either she will be out of cigarettes or she will tremble and wonder what to do with her hands. Either her chin will quiver pathetically or she will stand up straight and look Lance in the eye.

Either she will, in fact, arrive, or she will not.

Either Angela will protest the motion or she will not. Either the old woman will be heeded or she will not.

Gretta wishes she had not batted her eyelashes at her math teacher to get through statistics. Had she respected the gravity of probability, she might now be able to calculate the possibilities for a favorable return. The thought of crossing into the reservation now, under existing variables, doesn't seem promising so much as horrifying.

The first time Gretta went to the reservation, the probabilities, she feared, were not in her favor. Renee and Sylvia—Lance's mother and sister, respectively—had already expressed disdain and had recommended that she and Lance cancel the trip "until a better time." Lance was undeterred.

Gretta was to meet Lance's Aunt Angela, a serious Navajo, by the looks of her bun. James and Lance's youngest brother, Darrel, had shown her a picture: "The Navajo sense of humor is a little different. If she says anything, don't take it personally."

"We'll go find Erikson," Angela told Lance when they got there. Gretta thought she meant eventually. "You get that car ready. It's just down that road a ways and turn left." Angela looked old then, twelve years ago, like she looks old now, so Gretta was surprised.

"You sure, Mom? It's almost ten," Lance said.

"Mom?" Gretta asked. She wondered if he were adopted. Or if by *aunt,* Lance had meant *father's ex-wife* or something. Would there be, then, two mothers whose asses would have to be kissed for the occasional nod of approval? The thought was overwhelming. She nudged Lance's foot to get a look at him. Lance nudged her back. Firmly. She shut up.

She couldn't get in the way, she knew that. Lance had to get his whistle fixed. He would be strange until it was fixed, and she'd about had enough of that. After the eagle-bone whistle broke in his back pocket, he looked behind him everywhere he went. The whistle had broken the day he left home to move with Gretta to Salt Lake (Lance's mother, Renee, likes to remind her), and he'd been haunted by it ever since. At night he accounted for every creak of every door, every groan of the old pine floor of the bungalow that was their apartment building: "Who's witched me? It's Lawrence in Arizona—I owe him money. No, Jana in New Mexico—she doesn't like mixed marriages." Somehow, Lance's aunt was a vehicle for clearing it all up.

Angela reheated mutton, green beans, and fry bread for Gretta, Lance, and Angela's three granddaughters. She called for her husband, Jerry, and her son-in-law Randal. They said they weren't hungry, but they sat at the table to eat anyway and they watched Gretta. The mutton was cold by the time she knew what to do with it—chew small bites and spit them into a napkin, pretending to wipe her mouth after each bite. When the girls caught on, they tried it too, until Randal began to giggle.

"You don't like mutton?" Angela asked. Her consonants sounded like eggs falling off a counter, her vowels, the gasp that follows.

Randal and the girls watched and waited. Lance stopped eating and looked at Gretta, who hoped desperately the woman was referring to the half of the mutton steak on her plate and not the half in her napkin.

"I was saving it to go with my fry bread."

"Good. Because you're going to butcher me a sheep tomorrow." Randal stifled another laugh, but Angela's eyes would not leave Gretta's. "We'll go to Grandma Shiprock's and you'll get me one."

Gretta looked at Lance to read his expression: *She doesn't mean it.*

"You know how to butcher a sheep?" Angela demanded.

Gretta shook her head no.

"You got to cut its throat so the blood drains out."

Gretta dropped the napkin onto the floor. Her sweaty palm swept across her neck. The dog scurried over and ate the half-chewed pieces of meat. She heard laughter overlapping chastisement in Navajo. Eventually, her plate came into focus. The plate was of the same make her mother had years ago. It had a chip in it. Her knife was a good one. She closed her eyes and counted backward from thirty the way her caseworker had instructed.

She was afraid to face Lance, and when she did, she almost started crying. "I can't do this," she wanted to say. "I'm afraid, and I can't. I'm sorry." By the time she opened her eyes, Lance was looking at Angela too, to see if she was serious.

Gretta's resentment started then and kept going. She was told in AA that if you quit drinking, the disease will progress nevertheless. Then, when you start again, you drink like you never stopped, and your body falls apart accordingly. That's how she feels when she sees Aunt Angela.

"*Mom,*" Lance told her later in the hall, when she demanded an explanation, "that's like *aunt* in the Indian way. Don't worry—you'll figure it all out."

"I won't kill a sheep," she whispered.

"You don't have to kill a sheep."

"I will *never* kill a sheep."

"You don't have to kill anything."

"You'll have to kill the sheep. Or she—she will have to kill it herself."

"No one's going to kill anything." He grinned. "Not this weekend."

"Not so loud! I'm a hypocrite, I know."

"You're fine. She was joking!"

"I can never watch—"

"I'll make sure you never have to watch." He smiled at her, kissed her, and otherwise comforted her with small kindnesses.

After dinner, Gretta and Lance waited on the couch while Angela watched TV. Jerry left to work the midnight shift and everyone else went to bed. Angela sped through a few dozen channels. She stopped for a moment at Wonder Woman playing a settler in a series with American Indians. Gretta thanked god the actors playing the Indians were, at least, Indian, but the other shows—where was *Cosby* at least?—white, white, *pasty* white, white. When finally she turned her head to see the outrage, she saw not anger but boredom. That, and the faces of Lance and Angela seemed to have taken on a darker hue. Angela went through the mix several times, like a punishment. Gretta felt like she should apologize. She couldn't manage to speak to the old woman—couldn't change sitting positions, much less apologize for TV programming. Instead, she tried to imagine which of the eleven people who lived in the trailer house went to which of the two rooms to sleep—how many people could, in fact, fit in a little trailer house.

When Angela made motions of leaving, Lance and Gretta packed pillows and blankets in the backseat of their Civic for her arthritic body.

"Which way?" Lance asked as they pulled out of the gravelly trailer court.

"Turn that way, toward Window Rock."

Lance punched in a tape of Cathedral Lakes and turned the volume high. Gretta waited for Angela to get mad. The lead had an eraser-soft voice, but still, it was a northern song—high-pitched and demanding. Angela said nothing, looked out the window, her lips tucking under her nose and cheeks now and then. They drove about forty minutes that way.

"How far is it, about?" Lance asked.

"Just turn left when I say."

And then they drove some more.

Gretta had slept through most of the drive across southern Utah and into Arizona and it was dark when she woke up in Fort Defiance, so she could only imagine what the landscape looked like. Tall red buttes. Canyons curvy as ears. Sagebrush and sand. *Rabbits fucking rabbits—*

"Don't look out the window!" Angela snapped. "You might see something you don't want to see."

"There's those woofs," whispered Lance. Angela coughed.

Gretta tried to imagine Erikson, Lance's family's medicine man. Long glossy hair. Defined nose. Strong hands. Shoulders like Lance's, with indents like mouse bowls on top. *No, he'd have to be real old,* she thought—*Windwalker,* like. Lance had driven over nine hours to get to the reservation and had only a weekend to find him. The words *medicine man* ground against her nerves but she understood her disgust had little to do with the medicine in the man. It was the book—*Everything You Ever Wanted to Know about Crystals* by Shanli JudithAnne Hali, Medicine Woman. Gretta had mistaken it for a rock-hound's guide and fast became dispossessed of tangentiality, relegated as she was to a lower rung of an alternate version of ye olde Christian chain of being.

Lance had said there would be a fire. *Or was it coals?* There would be a fire pit, and Erikson would see things. She tried to think of a movie or a book involving an American Indian ceremony and a fire. She saw instead Frenchish black people in colorful billowing clothes. Her chest contracted. She didn't know anything about Navajos. She didn't know anything about Frenchish black people. It was true—she lived in a loaf of Wonder Bread under the conspicuous eye of a temple-topping bugle boy.

Gretta wondered what Erikson would do with the broken whistle. Maybe he would mend the two pieces together. *With what? Glue?*

Gum? Wintergreen Extra was what Lance had put on his whistle at a road stop on the way down, long enough to use it. And it was a good thing he'd had it, he said, because a coyote had crossed the highway going left to right. *Or was it right to left?* He had to make an offering or a request—she couldn't recall which—with Indian tobacco wrapped hastily in a corn husk. *Got to watch out for those woofs!*

Angela coughed again as if she were reading Gretta's thoughts.

"That left?" Gretta asked as they passed another left-turning dirt road. Angela didn't say anything. Neither did Lance.

Gretta stared at her lap. She stared at Lance's lap for a while. She thought about his pubic hair, which was straight. She hadn't known pubic hair came in straight until she met Lance. It is said that Navajo pubic hair stems from Mą'ii—the coyote that necessitated the tobacco. From the time she learned that, curly hair seemed hesitant, bent. Like the hair of sheep.

"Wooly, that's right," she says now, to an audience of none. Surely white women's pubic hair has been described as such. She has been described as such.

WordsforLater.doc

Woolly also wooly: Of, relating to, or bearing wool. Lacking in clearness or sharpness of outline. Marked by mental confusion. Marked by boisterous roughness or lack of order or restraint <Where the West is still *woolly* —Paul Schubert>.

Uncanny how the words call her to attention, decrypting her every inclination, her every contradiction, with more specificity than she herself could bring into shape. She likes to think of herself as a woman of little superstition, but she can't deny that the very eyes of the dictionary, or at least *her* dictionary, seem trained on her. *To what end? Why me? Why bother?*

"Thank you for calling Moab's own Golden Granary Pharmacy, where customers always come first. Para Español, marqué uno. To order refills by phone, press two now. To leave a message…"

Wherefore? Whyever? West what? Which West? Had she a dictionary to pack around with her the night they first went looking for Erikson, she might have been warned: she would always be the straw that broke the whistle's back. *Still wooly.* Even then she knew that on some playing field, she would always represent Christopher Columbus and the oxymoron of "discovering" a previously inhabited land. She would always be John Smith—not Smith of the Disney love-project *Pocahontas* or of Malik's pretty-pretty work of clitoratography, *The New World,* but Smith the mercenary, the wanderlust braggart who settled kidnappers and murderers on Indian land, bringing with him an as-yet eternity of disease, hopelessness, and death. There, deep in Navajo country, she would forever be Kit Carson, putting bullets in people's backs, forcing families from their sacred homeland, across three hundred miles of desolation, to something worse than the usual despair of a reservation—to a prison camp, really.

Had she carried a dictionary from the beginning, it might have warned her of a lot of things. *Colonist,* for example: *a member or inhabitant of a colony*. If the U.S. were a colony, wouldn't the ancestors of Lance, James, Angela, Erikson—all of Native America—by definition, by force, be colonists, the colonized and the colonizers being subsets of a larger group? For that matter, could she have denied the U.S. was still, in fact, a colony on the larger yardstick of time?

WordsforLater.doc

Colony: A body of people living in a new territory but retaining ties with the parent state: the territory inhabited by such a body. A circumscribed mass of microorganisms usually growing in or on a solid medium. A group of individuals or things with common characteristics or interests situated in close association <an artist *colony*>. A group of persons institutionalized away from others <a leper *colony*>.

Had she a dictionary, she would have understood the truth about language—the truth about her life: that neither historical accounts nor her personal proclivity toward contradiction could ever be reconciled.

Claims of fairness and sensibility may once have sat beside her, cast in bronze by way of taxpayers' money, but they were neither organic to the scene nor interactive with her personal picnic.

Of course, she wasn't warned. (Or, she wasn't *sufficiently* warned. *The Navajo sense of humor is a little different....*) She didn't own a dictionary then. Rather, she had school loans and bill collectors and notices from the library. She didn't have a medication either, much less a diagnosis, beyond Town Crazy Girl.

So there she had been, trying not to look out the windows of the Civic, feeling Angela's gaze as if it were her own, Carson-unawares. A Long Walk, not by a long shot. A long ride—*fuck yeah*. Eventually, she went to sleep. She was jolted awake by deep ruts in a dirt road. Gretta forgot Angela's warnings and looked out the window for some sign that they were close. They must have driven a long way because a different tape was playing, and Gretta couldn't see houselights anywhere.

"How far?" Lance asked.

"Just down this road," Angela said.

Plywood had been laid out over a rut too big to cross. There were trees, piñon and juniper she could smell through the windows—they were climbing higher.

A hogan and a rusting trailer house became visible around a bend in a flash of headlights. Gretta had seen a picture of a hogan before, but she never thought of it as a place people lived. Not anymore.

A couple of minutes passed. She waited for someone to appear at the wood-framed doorway of the angular dome of the hogan, or perhaps to emerge from the trailer. She whispered to Lance, "How will he know we're here?"

"If he's here, he'll come out," said Angela.

No lights were on. No cars were in sight. They waited for a long time. Gretta asked Lance if he should go to the door of the trailer and knock on it.

"I'm not going out there," he said.

Hello, Please Help Me

"IT'S ME. You up?"

"Good god, Gretta. What time is it?"

"Late. Early."

"You having another one?"

"She won't leave me alone, Grandma. I'm scared."

"She's not real, honey."

"My skin burns. I don't feel right."

"Just breathe. Say it isn't real."

"Okay."

"Out loud."

"She isn't real. But she wants me to do something. If I knew what it was, maybe I could do it and she'd go away."

"If she isn't real, there's nothing for you to do. It's that front globe, you heard the doctor."

Gretta inhales three seconds, exhales four. Inhales three—*exhale two, three, four.* Her grandmother doesn't protest the silence, doesn't try to break it.

Soon the images of the woman recede as inevitably as they came. The nausea grows.

Gretta says, "It's not the frontal lobe; it's the temporal lobe."

"You see? If you can tell me I'm wrong, you're all right."

It's clear her grandma has been researching seizures; Gretta's neurologist said nothing of the lobes of the brain, not when Grandma came with her, anyway. She wants to tell her she loves her for looking into it and ask her if she finally used her Internet connection or if she went to a library.

"It's going away."

"It always does. Have you been taking your pill?"

"I don't know. I don't feel right. I think I'm going to throw up."

"Are you sitting down? I think you should sit down."

"She's always there, Grandma. I saw it. Even when I'm not in it. Even after. Even before."

"Where?"

"I don't know. Dreams, maybe. She had a towel this time. Or a sheet. And brown hair—longish light brown hair. Can you remember that for me? And don't tell my mom. Don't tell her anything. Tell her I'm fine."

"Come home, Gretchen. Don't give your imaginary friend any more mind. Don't try to make sense of something that's not real. You ought to be in bed asleep by now anyway. Don't you have a room? You need some money, Button?" She waits at length for an answer; Gretta has nothing to offer. "And where do you think chasing Lance is going to get you? A seagull will eat anything you give him but you won't be able to catch him once you've thrown him a chocolate cake. And think about your health. A little mal today can be a damned big mal tomorrow."

"I don't think it works that way. Look, I feel real sick. I got to lay down. Maybe I need to sleep a bit. Call the kids, please. Check on them. Tell them I miss them. I really, really miss them."

She feels as though she will cry—out loud. Or laugh uncontrollably, which would be not only embarrassing but criminal, to some minds.

Her head hurts. Her shoulders ache.

"Jackie should have picked Tulip up from school by now, and Braden—can you check on them? Tell them I love them and I'll be home soon?"

"They know."

"Just in case, I mean."

"Of course I will."

"I'm sorry, Grandma. I love you."

"You take your pill, and call me next time—"

How to Make the World a Better Place

GRETTA DREAMED of trains, of trying to teach the upper torso of a man to swim. Not the fading dream-abstraction but the memory that must have prompted it washes over her. When she was ten or eleven or so—she can't remember exactly how old—her dad took her to the train yards. She'd gone to work with him more than a few times, but this time, they stood in front of an empty rail as he passed her a checklist. He pointed to an oncoming train and said, "Now, they're going to go by really fast. You look at the numbers in the lower corner of the car and just see that they're all there. You think you can handle that?"

What numbers? Which corner? She wondered what would happen if she missed a number—would a train wreck? Would her father be fired? Surely this must be a game, a way to keep her busy. She didn't dare ask. The engine approached; she looked for a driver and saw none. She saw that the numbers on the list started with letters. She started to ask whether letters were in this case numbers, but the question didn't make sense to her as the sound of the train fast grew overwhelming. She saw the first car and understood, felt stupid: a serial ID appeared, just as on the checklist. She was always getting confused like that—over semantics. But she didn't know the word *semantics* then, so to her the confusion was not a glitch in communication but intensely self-reflective, a daily horror.

She kept up with the list at first, matching a series of letters and numbers to each car, but the train began to move faster and faster and she missed a couple of cars.

"Right down that-away I once saw a man cut in half," he yelled over the deep rumbling and petulant screeching of the train. She tried to focus on the list and the cars but felt the severance in her gut. She missed about every fourth or fifth number. "That's right—poor homeless bastard. His legs too. Cut in thirds, I should say. Or fourths, if you're counting legs. Nice black fella. Used to have coffee together every once in a while, him and me. Then he'd just disappear for god knows how long."

She tried hard to make out the increasingly blurry IDs and popped her jaw open to plug her ears. She saw blood, bowels, a screaming black man.

"Wouldn't you know, he lived all the way to the hospital. The Dee had closed by then, and the new hospital was a ways away. Bagged up his glower darts myself in a trash bag and chased after the ambulance with them."

"What?" she shouted over the train.

"Said I bagged up his lower parts myself and took them to the hospital on the off-chance—course, they weren't able to use them."

She was missing so many IDs. Would cars be diverted to the wrong place? Would her dad be shamed? Whenever she met older men at the railroad, they held her shoulder or patted her head. "Your grandfather was a good man—the best kind, a real legend," they'd say. Her own father would wince, or she imagined he did.

"Yeah, lots of homeless down here. Where else they going to go?" He looked around the yard, as if for the first time. "Hey, I'll be up in the tower. Come on up when you're done."

With the last car in sight some dozen cars out, she screamed for him. "Wait!" She checked off the last of the IDs—most of them, anyway—and turned to him, the yard suddenly silent as a dip under water. "How come he didn't bleed to death right off?"

"Train's so heavy and so hot on the rails, it sealed him shut."

"Could he talk?"

"They say he was telling jokes all the way in." Her dad squinted at her—in anger, in curiosity? "An accountant is having a hard time sleeping and goes to see his doctor. 'Doc, I'm having a hell of a time trying to sleep at night.' Doc says, 'Have you tried counting sheep?' Guy answers, 'That's the problem. I make a mistake and then spend three hours trying to find it.'" He waited for Gretta's response, his face hard and creased. "Yeah, I guess it ain't that funny, but there's not a one of us who could do better under the circumstances."

Sheep. Why does it always come round to sheep? They're surprisingly stinky, sheep. And never quite as fully white—or black—as you'd expect.

Gretta boots up the laptop, cranks the heat on high, turns her cell-phone ringer back on, and checks her voice-mail. "Bill here. Let me ask you something, Gretta. What do women want to read? What do *normal* women want to read? You think about that question. Think about it and give me a call back, ASAP. And I don't want to hear anything about Gaza. I don't want to hear anything about levees or surveillance or places you can sneak into and shower for free—our readers have showers. Think women. Think your neighbors. Better yet, think *my* neighbors. Jeeze Louise, Gretta—think *Utah*. Think *Citizen*. I want June ready for layout by next week. Let's get ahead of the game." She replays the message to listen to the time stamp: 9:43 P.M. He called so late—for his habits, at least. "When I go home, I leave my work at work," he likes to say. Gretta tucks her worry away and considers his question. What *do* normal women want to read?

She finds a Zoloft in the console but nothing with which to drink it down.

Ideas.doc

1. How to look younger.
2. How to eat less.
3. How to tweeze.
4. How to make 101 varieties of holiday cookies.
5. How to raise children.
6. How to buy more for less.
7. How to be loved by a man.
8. How to be good in bed.

It occurs to Gretta she is neither the feminist she thought she was nor the revolutionary she had aspired to be. She offends even herself. Maybe a real publication would tell her exactly what women want to read (determined by a panel of, say, six), then she could just write about it, true or not. But working for a Mickey Mouse press like *Utah Citizen*...she doesn't dare ask.

`9. How to make the world a better place. By gardening.`

It occurs to her also that she is out of gin and the sun is just now rising. She wonders where and when she got her pajamas—penguin-print bottoms, a striped top. She has no clean clothes, as she accidentally left the suitcase with her clothes in it by the front door when she left home. She considers her surroundings. The sun in the east lights up the tips of the buttes to the west, strata by strata, transforming a gray wall of stone into a luminous sandwich of red-white-and-gold towers. The sky is clear blue and the stillness of the morning is merciless. She takes a photo of the buttes with her phone because she's out of film for the old Leica she inherited from her grandfather. The digital photo is blurry, so she stills her hand against the dash and takes another. Still, the image doesn't approximate the beauty of the light on the rock.

In front of the truck is a sign: Moab 5.

Five miles to Moab—why hadn't she just gone into town? And why couldn't she remember how she got here? If Lance were here, he'd rub her back as he had nearly every night for years, since an unfortunate laminectomy. He'd even sing her a song with the hand drum, if she asked nicely. *That, or he'd leave me again.* She wishes now she'd rubbed his flat feet after every back rub rather than just when he pouted.

She plugs her cell phone into the lighter and calls home. She has postponed the call as long as possible. She's been friends with Jackie for years, but her friend doesn't particularly like children, which explains, in part, why she doesn't have any. *So why leave them with her?* Jackie answers, groggy and irritated.

"*Hello,* I said. Hello?"

"I'm sorry, I didn't think you'd pick up this early. I was going to leave a message."

"Yeah?"

"It's taking longer than I thought. I'm sorry—"

"I told you it would. If he wanted to leave, he would've by now."

"I should be home late today."

"How'd it go?"

"Oh…I haven't seen him yet."

"You're kidding."

"You know, setbacks." Gretta tries not to cry.

"Do you want to talk about it?"

"No."

"You're going to need time to talk with Lance, you know. He's not just going to hop in the truck as soon as you get there…. You know, just because you want him to come home doesn't mean he's coming home…. Gretta, Gretta. Don't get your hopes up too high, okay? You're going to be fine with or without him. You've got me, right? You've got your kids. I mean, you've got yourself. You never know what you're capable of. I just ordered this great set of tapes—"

"I'm sorry."

Jackie heaves a throaty sigh. "Just as long as you're home by Friday. I have that date with Josh. Tu-tu and Braden are fine. We're having fun. We saw a movie last night."

"What'd you see?"

"Some damned thing. Kids' show. Talking dog, that kind of thing. Braden ate a whole bucket of popcorn by himself. He's still shitting kernels."

"I'll pay you back. I'm sorry."

"Quit apologizing. Did you or did you not arrange my mother's funeral? Just be home by Friday. Promise me."

"Promise."

"Keep in touch. Anytime *after* eight in the morning or before midnight. And Gretta, try not to go off on him. It doesn't help." She waits. Gretta has little to say, nothing to say it with. "You can always turn back. I mean, what do you stand to gain, really? You don't know where he's been. He could have herpes or hepatitis or something by now."

Jackie is right—Gretta would need to insist on tests. She would need to have the conversation she'd been skirting for so long. The conversation would have to begin with an accusation of some sort.

"Gretta?"

"Yeah, I'm here."

"I'm sorry. That was harsh."

Could you put the kids on the phone, please? That's what she wants to say, what she knows any decent mother would say. But she's having trouble focusing. *Herpes, AIDS, genital warts, the clap....*

"Hello? I think your phone is cutting out. Gretta?"

An accountant is having a hard time sleeping at night and goes to see his doctor....

"Uh-oh, I'm beeping. Sorry, Jackie, I think I'm running out of battery—" She snaps the phone shut and breathes deep, *two, three.*

She stuffs her jacket against the window, a reluctant pillow for a throbbing headache—*exhale two, three, four.* Eventually, she sleeps some more.

Just So You're All Right Now

THERE IS a tapping from the crane; Gretta wills it to go away. There is still the tapping. Or it isn't the crane, but the ground that taps. Gretta stirs under the bright light of day. She looks around. She is in the pickup; there is no crane. There are no tractors, no dirt roads, no construction sites. There is just the truck. There is just the tapping—the tapping at the window: a woman wearing a hat. Gretta rolls down the window a good eight inches before it sticks.

"Are you all right?"

"Oh, yeah. I guess I got sleepy."

"Just so you're all right."

"I am, thank you."

"I mean, your truck is running."

"Yes, thank you."

"And it looked like you were sleeping."

"Yes. My starter is broken."

The woman stares, appearing speechless.

"I said, *my starter is broken*."

The woman backs away, raises a hand as if to wave, smiles awkwardly. "Just so you're all right now."

Gretta raises her hand too, smiles in return, and rolls her window back up again.

The sun is high. A row of bikers pass on a bike trail to the right. *With a fraction of their ambition—*

Lance: "Why don't you take walks at night? Go jogging? If you exercised, you wouldn't need antidepressants." Her mother: "Get off the goddamned couch once in a while. Catch up on your laundry—you'll feel like a new woman." Her brother: "When you decide you're ready to stop sulking and bullshitting about seizures and sore joints, I'll *buy* you a mountain bike." Lance's sister: "I'm not exercising. I'm *athletic.* Don't you see the difference?"

Maybe she does, maybe she doesn't.

In only hours—*six? five?*—she will be standing in front of Lance, presenting some argument or another. She has imagined the moment many times. She sees the approach, the entrance, the look on his face, which varies with her mood. She opens her mouth, and…nothing.

"I've decided to quit drinking and I need your help," she could say. Or, "James suggested I come find you." *Yeah right.* That might elicit questions. Also, Lance might have heard from James more recently than she has. He might have gone on leave, made a call; they might have had a conversation. About her. Lance might have heard about their night on the town before James left. She's grateful now she didn't have sex that night. Not that she hadn't wanted to…. She stretches her fingers. *Just what kind of man falls for his brother's wife? Just what kind of wife entertains falling for him in return?* Her brain throbs larger with every thought, every question; she feels it will balloon out her ears at any moment, but she can't seem to stop. Why hadn't she told her husband about his brother's overtures, her own feelings? Or at the very least, why hadn't she simply cut off all communication with James, outside of powwows and other family functions? She'd made her choice when she married. And she had kids—they couldn't have interchangeable dad-uncles.

Until recently, she felt mostly okay with how she had handled the situation. She and James had been writing more or less weekly for years, even when they lived on the same continent and could have phoned. ("And how would that look on a phone bill?" she'd asked.) They'd never written about sex, and she'd never returned his affections—not explicitly, not since she and Lance were married anyway—so why should she feel guilty? Yet she'd got herself a P.O. box and paid for it every month in cash—not a sign of innocence, to her conscience.

Maybe James has finally told Lance about everything. Or more. Lance couldn't have found the letters, as she shredded all but the most recent. But if James told him about them, it might explain why she hasn't received a letter postmarked *Reagan* in over a month. Maybe it's why Lance stopped calling as well, even to speak to the kids.

At first she told the kids he'd gone to New Orleans to help rebuild power lines, phone lines, homes. Then Tulip started asking about their own leaking pipes, their plugged drains, the dishwasher that wouldn't work. Gretta had to come up with something else.

Your father is stranded in a hogan.... What? Yes, he's fine. Healthy as a horse.... Drive to a phone? I'm sorry, didn't I mention? Your father is on a spiritual quest in a hogan, way back in the backwoods—no driving allowed. Also, no phones.... What's that?... Of course he misses you.... How do I know? Through prayer. He spoke to me through prayer.... To you directly? I don't know, Tu-tu—pray and find out.

Eventually, she told them something closer to the truth. That he just left. *Why what?... I don't know. Why anything?* Somehow, Tulip seemed more contented with this.

Gretta puts the pickup in drive to check her gas gauge—she is still a hair above empty. *Time enough,* she thinks. The laptop's battery has run out. She unplugs the cell phone from the lighter and hooks up the inverter.

DearJames.doc

p.s. I didn't mean all the things I said before you left. If you never see me again, please let's keep it between you and me. I won't mention the letters if you don't. And if you do see me again...well, what's the use in telling?

All That Matters

"WHAT THE HAY is this, Gretta? Riots and bra burnings?"

Gretta pulls into the Golden Granary parking lot. "It's 134 words. More are coming." She hits the spacebar on the laptop to keep it from hibernating.

"Riots and bra burnings. Who's having riots and bra burnings? And the *Dilbert* financial page? That's not a source. That's a mockery, is what it is. Did you get my message?"

"Yes, I did."

"Have you thought about what I said—really thought about it?"

"Yes, I have. Look, I didn't want to say anything, but…it's Lance. They think he's dead." She produces a gurgle. She wonders how far she can carry it before Bill catches on or at least feels guilty for pressing on her duress. "I'm the only person who can—I'm sorry—identify the mole…on his left cheek."

"His what?"

"His *other* cheek."

"Ah, geez. I'm sorry. You should have told me."

"I haven't been myself. Just give me a little more time, please." She clears her throat, sighs audibly.

"Freaking-A, Gretta."

"Yes, Bill. I know."

"And let's not forget foods and gardening. I mean, if you think you can. I mean, he's been gone for a while, right?"

"Right. Foods. And gardening. It was on the tip of my tongue.

You have no idea." She sniffles again. She performs a strengthening of spirit: *plié, chassé.* "I'm your girl."

Prick, she thinks. Her husband is dead, and he wants foods and gardening. *But he isn't dead.* "Entirely beside the point," she tells herself.

"What?"

"I said, 'Good-bye, Bill. Thanks for believing in me.' I mean it. You don't know what your patience means to me. To me and my [*sob*] children."

Bill probably doesn't believe anything she says after the excuses she has given him: a mastectomy gone awry; a baby cougar rescued from the hands of her friend, a Tibetan poacher; a near-fatal collision with Bruce Willis in Park City; a burglar breaking into her bedroom to pray at her bedside. Basically, she likes to fuck with Bill and, at the very least, witness him exercising a full spectrum of pseudo swear words. She will, someday, punish him for her unrewarding career, a promotion for a non-Mormon woman being naturally out of the question in the land of Zion. The *other* land of Zion.

She hits the spacebar again. *Go ahead, go on in now.* She sees herself getting out of the car, walking into the store. But she doesn't get out of the car. She doesn't walk into the store.

Maybe she doesn't need the Dilantin. Maybe she's not having seizures—maybe she's just crazy or self-indulgent, as her brother suspects. So why pay the money? Why should she feel nervous and shaky and nauseous all the time? Why should she have sore gums? She could be suffering side effects for nothing. The episodes weren't necessarily *eliminated* when she took the medicine. *Maybe if you'd remember to take your meds every day....*

Perhaps it is the stress of her job—of hating her job—and not a neurological disorder that brings on hallucinations of the woman. Maybe she doesn't need a pill so much as an employment agency.

Writing reviews and other articles about spa specials, scrapbooking, ski resorts, and other such nonsense, she feels deeply misplaced. One day she will break out of *Utah Citizen,* never to hear the words *proactive, impactful, venue, team member, apres-this, apres-that,* or even *ambiance* again. She'll tell the finest chefs of Park City, Salt Lake, and, most deliciously, Deer Valley to go fuck themselves, just for the sake of balancing out the kiss-ass foodies looking for mutual admiration and free food. She's not sure what she'd rather be writing, but she feels certain that over the course of this job, she has given something up—something rare, something animate, something so nearly tangible, she is inclined to hold her breath until she grasps it again in all of its surely breathtaking familiarity.

Foods and gardening.

She doesn't cook. She doesn't garden (though the concept is novel, an aspiration). She would demand sports, on threat of sexual harassment, just to piss off the men, but she has witnessed, first-hand, college football players peeing on walls and bashing their heads into beer kegs; she refuses to anguish over the Utah Jazz any longer; she was ousted collectively from her fourth-grade soccer team, her sixth-grade softball team, and even from water aerobics for pregnant women; and she doesn't have the money to ski, not anymore.

Ironically, she is uniquely positioned among the all-white staff at *Utah* to write a column on cultural diversity (if there were such a column; there is not). She is an expert, after all, at standing in the margins of ethnicity and peering in.

She is also an expert at anticipating how much gin a 138-pound girl can drink before she fails to do her work, before daycare workers raise an eyebrow, before she slips down the stairs, before she gets her stomach pumped. But everything else—all that *matters,* as Bill would say—eludes her: fashion, landscaping, interior design, eating more for less, picking out a car, looking for a job, health and hygiene, beauty, family in the symbolic sense, travel.

Fuck Bill. She opens her laptop. A cop pulls up beside her. He parks, walks toward the entrance of the store. If she didn't reek of gin, if she had a valid license, she'd ask him where she could find a KOA—that is, a sink and a shower. *Then he'd know you weren't one of "our readers"!* She cracks open a pack of Tic-Tacs, boots up. If Lance were here, he'd know where to find a shower. He's never been one of *our readers* either.

Yes, indeed. She does love her husband in some respects, without hesitation.

June-gardening.doc

Summer Gardening

Spring is over and fdasajkl;fdsajkl;fdsajkl;fdsajkl;

She feels guilty leaving the truck running so long, particularly near the car parked in front of her, a Prius plastered with bumper stickers: YOU'RE GETTING WARMER; I'M A TREE HUGGER, I PINE FOR YEW; I ♥ MY MOTHER; and PLANT A TREE, REMOVE A BUSH. Speaking of oil, the price of gas is killing her, too—eating up the best part of the $190 she allotted herself for the trip. But she's not about to get stranded in a parking lot alone with a faulty starter, not now. Of course, she could just shut down, walk into the store, pay for her prescription, save gas. She isn't making progress with her article anyway.

In question is not so much what normal women want to read, but what normal women want to write. *So what would you write, if a woodchuck could chuck wood?* She couldn't say. Not without help. She withdraws a novel from the glovebox, opens it to the first dogear. The book is slim, precise, and soft from wear—just right. She braces it open against the steering wheel with the back of the screen.

TheLover.doc

So, I'm twenty-nine and a half.

It's on a cross of wheat and wheatgrass that I am tossed out of bounds.

The image lasts all the way across.

I'm twenty-nine and a half. There are four seasons in the southeastern part of Idaho, but I am suspended in one—hot, earthy—I'm on the berth of stupor, with nothing coming, nothing going.

I'm not allowed to photograph the sweat lodge, so I will not. I will tell you, though, it is hot, I am lost, it is wet, I am forbidden, and it is dark, I am told.

I can tell you about his body. I slept in it, I came in it or on it, whichever, it is a part of me. There is a type of photographic paper I like to use—satin, non-archival. The skin on his chest feels just like that. There is a distinct brittleness inside the chest: his ribcage is a sturdy old bridge, but it makes one wonder. It is hot, it is wet, it is the color of a brick house in the light of fiery pallets and glowing coals.

So, I'm twenty-nine and a half, there are four directions here—east, south, west, north—I walk through them all, around the coals, but I cannot say—

They told me to pray to Jesus. *Jesus?* I said. What of him. They say he walked on water. I say I sunk into earth. The coals were hot, forgive me, the steam scalded my skin, forgive me. Forgive me for trespassing, deliver me, in the name of the Father, the Son, and the Holy Ghost, and to the Republic, for which it stands, three Indian nations, under God, indivisible, I say these things in the name of Jesus Christ—

I said, *Who?* I said, *Pray to who?*

So I sank beneath the willows, lifted the carpet corners, breathed in the half-inch of cool air rising from the cold dirt beneath the sweat lodge.

They told me to pray to God, then. The Creator. *That higher power,* as they call it in AA.

I said, *Dear god, what would I say?*

I search for something to say in order to say it right. Everyone else seems to know how to say it right.

Nightcrawlers emerge.

I'm not ready. I'm sorry. Go down—down beneath the skin of the sky. Down beneath the skin of the lodge, beneath the skin of the carpets. That's where you'll find me—hot, earthy. I'm on the berth of stupor—

The Arc and the Sediment

GRETTA IS lost. She is surrounded not by redrock but by pine trees. She woke in her truck beneath a new-smelling, Christmas-colored quilt as the sun was beginning to set, then drove nearly twenty minutes down a shady canyon before her cell phone caught a signal. It's Tuesday. *Not Sunday—Tuesday. Night.* Parked on a two-lane road, wearing a godawful pink sweatsuit of unknown origination, she turns the light on in the pickup and flattens out wadded-up receipts against the seat.

Apparently, she made it as far south as a Conoco in Monticello on Sunday night before she turned around. By Monday afternoon, she had backtracked north through Moab (she bought *Desert Solitaire* from Arches Book Company) and got as far north as a Shell station in Helper. Where had she slept Sunday night?

She counts her Zoloft. It doesn't help; she obviously hasn't been taking them. She takes one now, swigging it down with a warm, watered-down Sprite.

She recalls roofs lined with rows of old tires. She recalls a pawn shop, doors locked. She has a receipt for a blanket, a travel case, two shirts, a sweatsuit, jeans, underwear, and socks from Kmart in Price; she can't read the date and time for the fry sauce smeared on it. She looks in the back of the pickup—two Kmart sacks and a suitcase. A receipt from Monday night for FunYuns, Oreos, cigarettes, and baby wipes from Shady Acres in Green River and another right after that from Arctic Circle. *No toothbrush?*

That's it—that's all the paper proof she has. Between Monticello and Helper, there is time that cannot be accounted for, so she might have traveled farther. She checks her cell phone—No Messages—and scrolls through caller ID for calls made and missed: Grandma Flint, Home, Unavailable. She checks her photos: Tulip and Braden eating cereal, the lizard, the buttes outside of Moab, a fork, a denim-covered leg. Whose leg, she can't tell. Late this morning she made it to a liquor store in Price—and this part she remembers clearly, suddenly—before deciding it was imperative that she find out what they mined for on Hiawatha Mine Road in the Manti-LaSal National Forest.

Rumor had it that Gretta's great-great-grandfather laid track in Hiawatha briefly until he picked up her great-great-grandmother in Helper, who'd been roughed up for hustling a guy from Butch Cassidy's gang, and escorted her north to Ogden. That was her family's only claim to fame. She had to have a sense of the place to decide whether the stories were closer to fact or to fiction, didn't she? Or, that's what she likely told herself.

She never found out what it was the miners mined—it was dark before she hit the forest. She did, however, emerge from Price with a wealth of Gilbey's and a key ring reading Sagittarius Makes My Heart Grow Fonder. Neither she, nor Lance, nor anyone else she knows, save Braden, is a Sagittarius. Why would she buy a toddler a key ring he could choke on? But the tiny pewter horse-guy is cool—explanation enough for now.

The clerk at the liquor store in Price asked to see her ID, thinking she was too young to buy alcohol. "Who would've thought," he said, double-checking her birth date. "Well, that's not *that* old.... Bitsilly—that's Navajo, ain't it?" She nodded. "My aunt's foster kid was a Tso, but his mom was a Bitsilly. You sure don't look like a Indian."

"I was adopted."

"Huh. I'm from Hiawatha just outside of here, and that's almost like being Indian, ain't it?" He laughed, showed her a map laid out beneath the Plexiglas of the cashier stand. "See here? Hiawatha. Born and raised." She acted impressed. "You wouldn't want to go for a steak dinner, would you? I get off here in about an hour."

Now Gretta wishes she had asked him if she could take the map—wishes she had taken him up on the steak, for that matter.

She gets out for a cigarette. The night air smells like turnips. The door wheezes shut. Gretta feels as if she is in a vacuum. The stars enhance this feeling, forming at once the arc and the sediment where the vacuum bag puffs out. Just before the burst.

I'm not afraid.

Lance has asked her not to go out without him at night. Especially not alone, not in the desert. "You never know what might be out there," he has said.

"What?" she yells. She has always wanted to yell like that—just out with it. But her voice sounds absurd. She hears it over and over in her head, as though she is saying it again and again for the first time, and each time it sounds like she has eaten a marshmallow and shouted *what.*

I said, you're not afraid.

Back in the car, doors locked and windows shut, she makes herself a gin-and-tonic and breaks open the package of Oreos, which reminds her how badly she could use a toothbrush. "Forgot your toothbrush again?" Lance, an avid toothbrusher, would say. "Figures."

Gretta wonders how she and Lance endured one another's differences long enough to get married. She liked sweet, he liked salty. She liked blues and grunge, he liked hip-hop and country. She was a slob, he was a clean-freak. She couldn't stand southeastern Idaho, where they both lived with their respective parents, he loved it. He had always lived there, she had since graduating college. Some things they had in common: they disliked porn, they slept in every chance they got, their favorite month was May, they loved fresh peaches, and they were chronically late to everything.

He had been late picking her up on their first date—a symbol, at that early stage, and not a tendency, so she left. She passed him on the way out of her subdivision and he chased her down until she agreed to get in his car.

The air was muggy for Idaho; she sweated in her new dress and thought of ways to tell him off. Still she hoped he would take her someplace nice. Instead he drove several miles into the darkness, into a field in the middle of fields, and stopped the car. He turned off the headlights and rolled down his window.

"Yell something," he said, clearly not afraid of the night at that time. "Anything."

"I'm not going to yell."

"No one's out here. No one will hear you."

"You'll hear me."

What happens, she thought, *in a field at night, where there aren't any roads?* There were no streetlights—just a badly paved road and field mice. She stared out the car window, considering possibilities. There were a lot of weeds.

"I'm not getting out of the car."

Lance got out of the car. A toenail moon and a thickening of stars made his long hair blue. There was something she wanted out of him in that light, and it bit into her lungs. She got out.

"Yell anything—'Hey you,' or bark like a dog."

"You bark like a dog."

He sounded nothing like a dog. Not even a hound dog. More like a camel, she thought. She'd never heard a camel, as far as she could remember, but she watched one once at the zoo. For over a half-hour, the thing ate, stood, and pissed—all the usual camel things, she assumed—before it finally looked at her. It looked directly at her and held her stare until it went back to eating, its underside muddy and matted.

"Come on," he said.

"You can't make me."

"Yeah? I have the keys. Now relax. Look around. It's so big. You'll never get this kind of big if you move to a city, you know?" She thought he was nodding toward sex, a consolation prize for the seafood linguini she obviously would not be treated to that night, so she squeezed his hand and tried to kiss him. He didn't react.

"See how you shouldn't move to Salt Lake?" he said. "You can stay in Idaho. It's safe here."

"I hate Idaho. I've hated it since my dad dragged us here." She was a transplant, moved from Salt Lake City to Pocatello, Idaho. But her internship with Idaho State was up, and Idaho seemed to have little use for writers. She couldn't bear to graduate from college only to go right back to waitressing. She was the worst waitress she had ever known—the spill-coffee-in-your-lap kind of waitress, the I'm-sorry-I-forgot-you-were-here kind of waitress. And she had a job in Salt Lake writing newsletters, got for her by a friend of her parents. She had, it appeared, a destination. She had, as her mother would say, a *real* jay-oh-bee.

"Can't you feel it?" Lance asked. "Can't you just yell something like you want to be alive?"

Gretta can't remember whether she wanted to be alive then. It's doubtful, given the odds. She gets out of the truck again. She burns through her fifth consecutive cigarette and feels tired and hungry and weakened by destination. The sky, so porous with glistening stars, so sweetly devoid of human interruption, fills her with the sort of love that makes her chest contract and her nails grow fast—so fast, they tug fiercely at her fingers and threaten to make her cry.

There's no telling what happens in the sky. If you're dropped off a spaceship, do you float until you starve or till you freeze? Once, watching a James Bond movie, she saw a man locked in a vault. The air was sucked out instantaneously; the man's head exploded to watermelon size due to sudden lack of pressure.

"I'm not afraid," she says, studying the dark for difference. "I'm not afraid."

A Sore Cursing

"YEAH, HI. I'm just...I'm a little lost, and I was wondering—"

"Who is it, hon?" calls a woman from inside.

"A woman. Says she's lost," the man at the door shouts. He rubs a trim brown beard and spare moustache. He looks her up and down as a security guard might. She sees herself as she imagines he sees her: pink and puffy, corpse-pale, greasy, frazzled—the Easter bunny on meth.

"Well, invite her in. It's colder than a witch's tit out there tonight."

He hesitates only a second more. Her tennis shoes, she notices, are relatively clean but coming apart at the seams and her laces are different sizes. The man doesn't seem to notice the shoes.

She isn't sure what she should do with her hands. She sticks one out. "I'm Gretta. I won't sell you Tupperware or anything. I'm just lost."

He shakes her hand with some trepidation. "Come on in. You want to use our phone?"

She could tell him she has a phone, but it's cold out, and the house smells like Thanksgiving. She nods.

"We just finished with the blessing, but you're welcome to come in and join us for dinner. You hungry?" A refusal is out of the question; Gretta is painfully hungry.

"You want to wash up?" He says *warsh* instead of *wash*, just like her father. He waits outside the bathroom door while she *warshes* her hands and finger-brushes her teeth. His wife joins him; he chastises her for using obscene language in front of the children.

Gretta is ushered into a dining room where eight children—two boys and six girls—are seated. All are introduced. She half covers her mouth as she thanks them, knowing that if she doesn't smell like an ashtray, she smells like a bottle of gin. Yet by the time carrots and roast beef make the rounds, she has told them she once worked as a cafeteria cook for the Red Cross ("Not a cook, really—mostly I just washed potatoes, beans, rice..."), that she trained a parrot to sing "Goodbye Yellow Brick Road," that her grandmother in Arizona is sick and she is going to visit and care for her, an immigrant from the Netherlands, that—

"Bitsilly. That doesn't sound—"

"I'm married. It's a Navajo name."

"Delightful!" Nancy, the mother, says, clapping her hands together. The boys giggle. She introduces everyone at the table. "We were just talking about the Lamanites. Weren't we, Joseph? We once had one in our own ward. John something or other."

"Be *gay*," says the younger of the boys; they snicker. Their mother delivers a warning look to the oldest. They shut up.

"John Begaye. A proud man. A proud people," she says to her oldest son. "Go on, honey. Share with us their trials and tribulations with the Nephites."

The boy, Joseph, looks imploringly at his mother.

"Go on."

"There...there was this guy, Lehi, this Jewish guy—"

"Merchant. Jewish merchant."

"And he had these sons Laman and Nephi. And their descendents, the Lamanites and these Neo—"

"Nephites, honey."

"And then there was these wars, and the Lamanites and the Neophites—Nephites—fought a lot because the Lamanites just wouldn't listen, and then the Nephites died 'cause they were for Jesus."

"Why don't you just quote the scripture, Son," his father says.

"You'll need it next week," adds Nancy. "Samuel, please chew with your mouth closed. Darla, let's keep our hands to ourselves. Go on, Joey. Second Nephi, chapter five, verse twenty-one."

She whispers to Gretta, "Church pageant. He plays three different roles, if you can imagine that. Smart young man, this one."

"Mom...."

"Go on, Joseph. Listen to your mother."

"And he had caused the cursing to come upon the Lamanites. Yay, even a sore cursing, because of their indickity—"

"Iniquity," his father says.

"Wherefore, as they were white, and exceedingly fair and delightsome, that they might not be exciting—"

"Enticing."

"...enticing unto my people the Lord God did cause a skin of blackness to come upon them."

"And?"

"And thus saith the Lord God: I will make them—"

"Cause that they shall."

"...cause that they shall be loadsome—"

"Loathsome."

"...unto thy people, save they shall repent of their inlickety."

"Iniquity," Stuart, the father, says. "Very good. Practice makes perfect. Next time you'll do better, and the next time after that." He smiles encouragingly at Gretta as if it is she whom he has addressed. "You should see him pitch. They called him the Little League pride of Emery County at one time. When he started, he was on the bench. Go ahead, Joseph. Tell her the rest."

Joseph looks terrified. He looks as if he might be sick but takes an enormous bite of food.

"Can I play the piano for her?" begs one of the girls, who looks to be Tulip's age. Gretta tries to remember her name. Her mother mouths, "Later."

Sarah—the middle-sized girl, by the height of her—wrinkles a tiny bulbous nose and glares at Gretta. "Cause that they shall be loathsome unto thy people, save that they shall repent of their iniquity.

And cursed shall be the seed of him that *mixeth* with their seed…"

"Sarah!" Nancy says.

"…for they shall be cursed even with the same cursing. And the Lord spake it, and it was *done*."

"Sarah!" her mother shouts; she slaps the Formica table. She laughs nervously and smiles at Gretta. Stuart briefly appears exasperated but goes back to cutting his roast beef.

The girl lowers her voice, stares instead at her mother. "And because of their cursing, which was upon them, they did become an idle people, full of mischief and subtlety, and *did* seek in the wilderness for beasts of prey."

"That is enough! Do you want to go to your room?" Stuart says.

"I'm sorry, I should go. I need to find a hotel as soon as I can—"

"Please…it's so late. You can stay in Darla's room—can't she, sweetie?" Nancy gives her oldest daughter the same warning look she gave Sarah, but the look is unnecessary. The girl nods excitedly and smiles at Gretta. Sarah elbows her, but Darla scowls back at her sister.

Stuart clears his voice, glowers at his wife.

She glances threateningly at him then says, "For inasmuch as ye do it unto the least of these, ye do it unto me."

Stuart takes a deep breath, assesses Gretta as if with pushups. It is possible his belly too is blue, but unlike the lizard, he would not make a good souvenir for Tulip, and Gretta hopes never to bother his tail. He composes himself, looks regretful, even. "Of course you're welcome to stay."

After dinner, Stuart goes downstairs to watch TV. The kids fight over who should clean up; a couple of them do their homework in the kitchen. Their mother—"Originally Nancy Albertson, like Albertsons the supermarket?"—shows Gretta a shelf of scrapbooks she and her husband and children have put together, as well as her craft wall. "My Aunt Gladys is good at the butterflies, but my mother makes the doll babies. Aren't they precious? Sarah helped with this one." Gretta nods. Nancy fingers the objects hung on the wood-paneled wall—pink-blue-and-white crocheted butterflies and doll heads mounted on multicolored crocheted circles, not entirely unlike the elk head hung over the lava-rock fireplace at the end of the room or the mountain-lion head over the toilet in the bathroom. "They're like doilies, but with the doll heads in the middle. I'd like to make them, but…$3.99 a head at the craft store? Outrageous. They gouge us like crazy here."

"Where do you go to buy stuff?"

"Oh, Price. Helper. Sometimes we just drive over to Provo or Salt Lake during the holidays. I'm from Salt Lake, too. Moved here in '83 after we got married. My dad teaches economics at Salt Lake Community College and my mom teaches urban planning at the University of Utah. My brothers are all into computers. I myself graduated from Granite High with straight *A*s. Lot of good that'll do me out here." Nancy smiles—not sadly, not cynically, not happily either.

Unsure of how to respond, Gretta touches the doll-head doilies, too. "They're so…wow! The work your mother must have put into them."

"It doesn't take much." Nancy looks at her funny. "You need some more cough medicine?"

"What?"

"That's NyQuil, by the smell of it." Gretta senses that Nancy is feeling her out, soliciting a confession, but she plays along.

"Oh—" Gretta coughs. "Please, yes. This cold. It just hangs on and on. I hope it doesn't spread—I think I'm over the worst of it. I don't have a fever or anything. But…I really appreciate your thoughtfulness."

After Nancy returns from the kitchen with a tiny plastic cup, apologizing for having only generic cough medicine, she asks Gretta to have a seat. Gretta accepts the cup, pauses before drinking to see if the woman will call her bluff.

"We all had flu shots this year. Useless—we all got sick over the holidays." She sits across from Gretta on the edge of an afghan-covered recliner. "Are you a church girl?"

"I'm not." Nancy's brow furrows in something that looks like empathy. "But I'm looking into it," Gretta adds. *Practice makes perfect.* She lifts the cup, *cheers,* and drinks.

The woman nods, smiles. "I wasn't always. It helps, though. Out here." She yells at the kids, who are washing dishes in the kitchen, to get to bed. "I don't know what you'd do otherwise." After an uncomfortable silence, she adds, "I'm sorry about what I said earlier."

"I don't mind you asking. I'm used to it—I live in Utah."

"I mean about the witch's…breast."

Colder than a witch's tit—Gretta remembers now. "No, please. I thought it was funny."

"Maybe tomorrow we can talk more. Ham and flapjacks? We got a late start on supper tonight. What with the calving. It didn't go quite right. You know what I'm saying. The kids—we're all upset. Even Stuart, bless him." She shrugs, but her eyes glisten with tears. "These things happen."

She shows Gretta to her room. "Darla's got her own room now. She's ornerier than a cat in the rain these days. We said, 'You bring in at least a three-oh and shape up that attitude of yours, and we'll clear the sewing room out for you.' And you know, it worked. *And* she helps me around the house." She brings her voice to a near whisper, "These kids—I never knew it would be so hard."

Gretta sits awkwardly, wondering how she should respond. "You mind if I bring in my laptop, do a little work?"

"Your what?"

"My laptop. My—you mind if I bring my things in?"

"Oh, laptop! Whew! I thought you said something else. Can you get on the Internet with that from here?"

"Sure. Well, actually, I think I might be out of range on my cell phone."

"You got dialup, then?" Gretta nods. "Photoshop?" Nod. *Photoshop, Why?* "You can just unplug the phone and hook up in the kitchen. Even Darla's got a phone jack."

Gretta thanks her, tries to excuse herself.

"You think I can check my e-mail tomorrow?" Nancy asks.

"You can check it now, if you want. Would Stuart like to check—?"

"He doesn't care for computers. Anyway, he'll turn in after *The Apprentice.* He gets up so early."

Gretta returns with the laptop and shows Nancy how to select the eight-hundred number on dialup. Nancy shows Gretta the linen closet and the shower; she apologizes profusely for the bathtub being out of order. "You fill that big iron tub up and it'll fall right through the floor. Mildew. Wood rot. I keep telling Stuart, you're letting the house fall apart. I'll tell you this much, my mother wouldn't have put up with it." She puts a hand out but stops short of resting it on Gretta's shoulder. "I'll bet you wouldn't put up with it."

I'm above ground, aren't I? Still in the flesh? "You'd be surprised."

Hello, Kitty

THE BATHROOM smells of kitty litter and hot dogs, but the hot water seems endless and the water pressure is great. Once Gretta's hair is washed, she lies down in the bath. The shower rains down on her until cold water wakes her up. She dries off quickly, shivering, and wraps her hair in the towel. She curses the water that has somehow dampened one leg of her sweatpants.

Darla's room is decorated in Hello Kitty products—Hello Kitty bedspread, Hello Kitty posters, a ceramic imitation of Hello Kitty on a foldaway sewing desk. Above her bed is a picture of Jesus ripped from the church magazine *Ensign* and a small collection of spoons: Utah, Nevada, Grand Canyon, Colorado, Arizona, Capitol Reef, the Seagull State, the Beehive State. This room smells of old lace and faintly of mac-and-cheese—an improvement from the bathroom, but unsettling nevertheless. The laptop is sitting on the bed with a note: *Thanks!! We'll go over directions in the morning!* Gretta unplugs the sewing machine and plugs in her laptop.

June-Food.doc

Pakistani Burgers

2 pounds ground beef

½ onion

1 clove garlic, minced

1 Tbsp olive oil

1 tsp cinnamon

¼ tsp cloves

¼ tsp ginger

½ tsp salt

½ tsp black pepper

Mix ingredients and form into meatballs. Skewer and grill over medium heat. Alternative: Serve between pita bread or buns.

She checks her phone. She is in range, after all; she wasn't in range just a mile or two up the road. She considers calling her kids but worries she'll wake Jackie. She's also worried they'll ask why she's not home yet, when she's coming home. They'll wonder where she is. She will wonder where she is. If they're having a tough time sleeping at night without her, she'll have woken them up and made it harder on them and Jackie. She checks her voice-mail ("Gretchen, this is Renee—") and snaps the phone shut.

"The people will keep their eye on you. They'll watch how well you take in their ways," Renee told her one night when they were camped out at the Sho-Ban Festival. "They say in the old days the Indian people would capture the white women, and the women liked it so much that when they had a chance to go back to their own people, they chose not to. They stayed with the people. They liked it that way. You can do that too. If you follow that red road, then slowly by slowly, they will accept you."

Accept me, my ass, thinks Gretta. She knows she has never asked the right questions—that she misses the point by the act of asking questions. She waits for the knowledge to be gifted to her, but it doesn't come, and she grows anxious. The questions ulcerate until she can't take it anymore.

June-gardening.doc

So You Want to Plant a Garden and Spring Is Over

Spring is spent. You took a little trip, cleaned

> the molding, and ~~lay in bed recognizing shapes in the texturing.~~ worked long hours. Your intentions were good—plant a garden, get sun, eat well—but by the time you ~~stumbled into~~ visited the nursery, you saw that the colorful planting charts on the back of all the packets of seeds reveal the planting season to be over, or at least ~~inconveniently~~ suspended until after August. But all is not lost. ~~All is never lost.~~

And then there was the fact that she had to sort through Lance's *ways* to figure out which ones were acceptable to discuss with Renee and which ones were not. The night Renee had urged her daughter-in-law toward "that red road," Gretta made the mistake of thinking such *ways* were all open for discussion.

She had tried all summer to talk Lance into taking her to a 49 so she could meet his friends and cousins; they had been dating for a few months and still she had not been introduced. That August night, after the powwow, Lance refused her again. He said he had to go to the john and disappeared for a couple hours. Gretta asked Renee if Lance had gone to the 49 without her. Renee wondered tersely if she knew what a 49 was, as if offended Gretta would suggest her son went to 49s. Gretta didn't, in fact, know what one was—not exactly—but she did know from elliptical anecdotes that Renee's son had gone to plenty and had had some crazy-good times.

Lance returned to the trailer at about four in the morning; he and his mother argued until dawn. Neither of them spoke to Gretta for the remainder of the powwow. James came to her rescue the next day, taking her to the Fort Hall Trading Post for ice cream, then to the rodeo grounds near the powwow.

"You've got it all wrong," James said as they watched a rodeo queen make her rounds. "It's not that they don't accept you. It's that they don't know you. You always think everyone hates you. But maybe some of them are just thinking real hard when they look at you. Maybe they have heartburn. Maybe they don't feel like smiling all the time, like white people do." He looked instantly apologetic, blushed. "Except you, I mean. Anyway, my mom probably wouldn't care if we went to 49s. It's just singing and dancing and stuff. Mostly. I mean. Well."

That night, James showed her some of the horses—his friend's horses, anyway—groomed but still sweating, captive and worrisome. James kissed her then—not a little kiss, more of a bite without the teeth. It scared her, alone with him in near-dark, her loafers steeped in horse piss, and she ran, unable to watch out for shit, and she slid, caking one leg of her pants in manure. She walked and ran and tripped all the way back to the powwow grounds a mile or two away.

She returned smelly and sweaty as the horses, feeling both afraid that the kiss hung around her shoulders like a cheap scarf and victorious that now Lance and his mother really had reason to scorn her. The closer she got to the drum where he sat singing, though, the clearer she saw that he had not noticed her absence. It was guilt and fear that brought her back to Lance and shame that returned her to the tent to change pants, to hide the stinky ones in a grocery sack and throw them away.

She saw James at the arena later, as the flags were retired for the night. She apologized for running away. He seemed terribly embarrassed, apologized for the kiss, said he'd watched her to make sure she got down the road okay. "I would have picked you up and given you a ride, but I thought maybe you'd be mad." She wished she hadn't ran. She wished he had stopped to pick her up. Maybe if he hadn't chosen horse piss as a spot for a first kiss…maybe if she weren't so afraid of being confronted by her mother-in-law for something more than desire….

She imagines Renee watching her and James the night before he left for the Gulf.

A waste of fear, Gretta thinks now. *Should have learned how to rock climb instead.* Years have passed. A marriage and two children later, the only level of acceptance or understanding Gretta has really felt from her mother-in-law has come in terms of silence, in terms of degrees, by which she is dissembled.

She Googles "summer planting" for more ideas.

June-gardening.doc

You can plant, even in the ~~dry hot sun~~ summer. Here are a few seeds to stock up on for your June reunion with the ~~black tarry~~ earth:

Bush beans

Sweet corn

Cucumbers

Beets

Carrots

Turnips

Wando peas

Chard

Lettuce

Bok choy

Scallions

Broccoli

Cabbage

Brussels sprouts

If only Gretta could see her life in Track Changes. Through all her backpedaling, her comings and goings, through illusion and disillusion, her white lies and self-deception, she is unable to sort out what has been ~~deleted~~ from her story, what has been inserted, and most importantly, what `remains`.

DearJames.doc

p.p.s. It's not that I didn't like your little gesture. I mean, he's your brother. How was I supposed to react?

Someone knocks softly; Gretta opens the door a crack.

"Can I come in?" Darla whispers, standing in the hallway in a long nightgown.

"Of course! Your room."

"I wanted to show you something. I mean, Mom told me you're a writer and all, and I just wanted to show you." Darla closes the door behind her.

"Okay."

"But you can't tell, promise?"

Gretta loves a secret. "Let's see what you got."

She sits on the bed; Gretta sits beside her. "I have sketches and then poems. One drawing per a poem. I've been doing it since the fourth grade, but no one knows—not yet, anyway. One day I'm going to be famous like you."

"Oh, I'm not famous. I write junk. Swill. Dumb stuff. For a stupid newspaper."

Darla blushes, seems not to believe her. "Well…can you take a look and tell me what you think? But don't tell anyone."

A self-portrait on the first page reveals Darla to be a little older and have fuller lips, but the drawing is fairly good—much better than Gretta expected. "Your hair is straight here."

"I got a perm last fall. Big. Mistake. Mom left the solution on too long."

"This is really good. I like the eyes—they look just like yours. Such pretty eyes. Strong, perfect cheekbones."

"Thanks!"

Gretta wants to make a few suggestions, given that the girl has real potential, but decides it is not her role to play. "Have you taken art classes?"

"Yeah. Art *class.* At school. My teacher says I'm pretty good."

"She's got that right." Gretta smiles.

On the back of the page is a poem. Darla takes the drawing journal and reads the first lines before handing it back to Gretta.

Mi Amore

The air was cold as night

As sweet as a rose was by sight

And when she snuck out the window

He held up a flashlight

Gretta reads through the rest of the poem, nodding her head, reaching for comments. "You really rhyme. And the part on the baseball field—how romantic that must have been!" *Not your role. Not your role.*

"Darla?" her mother calls.

"Just getting some socks!" she yells back. "This house is freezing!" And to Gretta: "It didn't really happen that way. I mean, I made it up. I never did stuff like that. Jorge never did anything wrong. He's very nice, and he would make a great dad. I probably shouldn't write stuff like that."

"Come on, it's a poem. Tell the truth when you feel like it, make up the rest, is what I always say. I'll bet if you could see your parents on a baseball field twenty years ago.... Hey, you've got school tomorrow, don't you?"

"Wait! There's more." She keeps a watchful eye on the door. "You can read it. Silently."

Hate

I squeeze my teddy bear tight

And a lone tear runs down my eye

They made me turn off my light

Then Daddy came in

And scared me again
And one day I'll take flight
Set off in the middle of the night
Then Mom will cry
And wish she hadn't let him hit me
She'll be sorry uptight
And that's all right
Cuz I hate her tonight
And I hate my dad too
And I don't know what to do.

Gretta racks her brain for something to say. Part of her wants to giggle, in the way that she giggles when almost being hit on the freeway, or when her grandma says *pussy* or talks about imminent death, or when she has been caught doing something cruel, like swapping out a guy's box of paperclips with a box of fumigated Box Elder bugs.

She tries to recall the vocabulary and mechanics of adolescence. More specifically, she wonders how long it would take for police to get over here—if they would even believe her account of the poem…her *interpretation* of the poem, they'd no doubt remind her. She couldn't hand over Darla's poems anyway—that would be a betrayal.

Maybe the parents would surrender the girl to Gretta. "I could use a nanny—I'll send her pay home for you to keep safe," she could say. *Of course. Surrender their daughter to a crazy drunk wearing a pink sweatsuit. Who doesn't go to church. Who has no pay to pay.*

"That's…you know what? That's a lot better than *my* first poems. And these sketches! I mean, this is good stuff…a unicorn and a…sword, and a rose."

"That's a clam. I mean, oyster. Like what pearls come in. See the pearl?"

Clearly Darla's forte is portraiture.

"So are you guys serious, you and Jorge?"

"Oh, we've been going together for running on two years. Since the seventh grade. No one knows it but us and his brothers."

"And the thing with your dad?"

"Oh, that's nothing."

"Scares you again—"

"That's just he gets mad sometimes."

"Does your mom know?"

"Some of it. Not all. No, she'd freak out if she knew everything."

Gretta doesn't know where to start. The woman appears in a flash but stays at a safe distance. *Inhale two, three. Exhale two, three, four....* "Let me ask you something. Something personal? Has anyone ever told you about, say, birth control?"

"Like, the pill?"

"Yeah, like that. Or condoms. Or both."

"I already went to the county health. I got the shot. Just in case, I mean."

"Okay, good. You got computers at school?"

"We got one at the library."

"You use e-mail?" *Inhale two, three...exhale....*

"Sure. You want to see my MySpace site on your laptop? I'll put your picture on my site, if you want. I could make you up a page if you don't have one, and you could put my picture on your site. Then we'd both just click on each other's pictures and—"

"I'm not very photogenic, Darla," Gretta says, writing her e-mail address on the girl's palm. *Inhale two, three...exhale....*

Go ahead and drop a line if your dad is molesting you, Gretta wants to say, but she could be completely wrong—the man was nice. If she were wrong, the girl might ask, "What does *molesting* mean?" *Awkward.* Maybe if she corresponded with her, the girl would open up and at least have the benefit of an outside opinion on things.

And what kind of advice would you give? The woman pushes near, refuses to weigh in. *An excellent point,* Gretta thinks; who is she to give advice? *Inhale....* But she could send links to any number of resources—*exhale two, three, four*—information to survive the horror of youth and sexuality for the next couple of years. Maybe, with help, Darla could turn eighteen without permanent damage, or maybe the girl would run away before then and look Gretta up for help.

Were you able to save yourself from permanent damage? She could be worse off: she could have life-threatening STDs. *"You don't know where he's been."* Maybe she has already contracted something from Lance; they had sex together only five months ago.

The aura has gone away before the seizure—and with it, the woman—but not the nausea. And not Darla.

Depo-Provera, she decides, is inadequate for the girl. While Gretta feels useless in protecting her from her father, she can say something: "Remember this, if you remember anything: nothing prevents festering, ulcerating, incredibly painful, permanent, open, and visible sores on your vagina like a condom. Write to me anytime and I'll write back. It'll be our secret. Anything you say will be our secret."

The girl, wide-eyed, thanks her, then slips out the door with her journal, stopping to say, "Sorry about Sarah. She's just mean like that. And...I don't think you're going to get dark skin, just because you're married to a Lamanite. Just so you know."

Gretta moves the nightstand in front of the door when she's sure Darla has gone to bed. She takes one of James's letters out from the dictionary and unfolds it, careful not to let it tear. She reads, though already it has been embedded in her brain.

Dear G.

Happy Valentines. Or at least I hope you get this in time. We never know when mail will go out. The mail system sucks—you'd think by now they could have made it better. Thanks for the dictionary—I'll try harder to spell better from now on.

You asked me what I think of it all. I think it gets lonely here. I get sick of these guys. It is so dam hot. I thought it was hot on the rez. This is a different kind of hot, the kind I hope I never have to feel again.

I know you think I am just a kid with a crush, but I have felt this way a long time and I am not that much younger than you either. My question is, did I do something wrong? I am sorry I went too far before I left. I just knew I was gonna miss you. How many times can I tell you that? And last time I came home, Lance was gone, and you still would not let me in, so I did not know when I would even see you again. I will tell you this again, Gretta, he is seeing someone else. I know him. Of coarse he cares about you, but he has got other plans.

Guy who jerks off all the time below me left his filthy sticky sock out—the one he wipes himself up with. Our names are written on our socks, so I made a flag out of it and hung it up in the washroom for everyone to see. You want to know the funny thing? His last name is Cox, so that is what was on his sock. Dumb ass still jerks off three times a day, even with people around. I think he needs prof. help. I think they need to get rid of some of the nasty dirty magazines around here—you can barely find a place on this ship that does not have beaver shots staring up at you.

Sometimes I wonder what we are doing in this country. It gets old. I fucking hate the Navy. I guess it could be worse. I could be in the Army or the Marines. Barker—I told you about him? The one who used to run his Dad's coffee shop?—he says his brother is in the Army and he got a serious wound to his head and lost his hearing and messed up his feet. His baby died about the time he got shot so they sent him home—for three weeks!!! And then they sent him right back again. Fuckers.

Can I come over when I get back in August? I promise I wont try anything. I just miss you and the kids.

Love, James

p.s. I think if you want to take the pottery classes, you should do it. What do they know? They said photography was too expensive too, and look at you now. You ought to just quit the paper and take pictures of people.

Or, I guess, make pots for them. Why don't you take Tulip with you to the class? She will love it. I will send you some money if you need it. If you need something else too just tell me.

In her last letter, Gretta forgot to explain the dictionary she sent James as part of his birthday present. She feels terrible about how he understood the gift, and since she didn't refute him in the last letter, she's sure he still thinks she wants to correct him. James spells okay, for the most part—he was an honor student in high school and in his year and a half in college, just like Lance. Mostly he just abbreviates the way a billboard might—he writes *hi* instead of *high*, *thru* instead of *through*, *U-R* instead of *you are,* and so on—or he did before he received the dictionary, anyway. She would never want to make him think she wanted to correct him, though. She just wanted to give him a bit of her own solace—he always sounded so disheartened.

She enters Google to pull up the day's military casualties. *All clear, Doctor.*

DearJames.doc

p.p.s. It's not that I didn't like your ~~little~~ gesture. I mean, he's your brother. How was I supposed to react?

I didn't send a dictionary so you would check your spelling. I only sent it to you because I thought you might like it.

Footsteps approach her door. She waits; nothing happens. Footsteps recede.

June-gardening.doc

Tips: In the summer, rain tends to be sporadic and heavy and lacks the consistency of the frequent light rains of spring, so you have to compensate with twice-daily watering until the plants are well-established. Also, you must plant the seeds deeper than you would in spring to keep them moist and cool. ~~foul-weather friends.~~

She saves, hooks her laptop up to Darla's jack, dials up. She hits Send, wonders if it's enough to keep Bill at bay.

She takes off her shoes and turns down the covers.

Whoop. Wu-hu...hoo. Whoop. Wu-hu...hoo. An owl—*burrowing owl? Spotted owl? Barn owl?* Lance would be in a minor panic. Luckily Gretta is not afraid. The owl is just an owl—her favorite bird, before she met Lance; for her, the owl is not a messenger of bad things to come. It is not an agent of people's bad intentions.

So why is her breath short and her body tense? *Whoop. Wu-hu...hoo.*

Spotted owl. So why is she gathering her things and putting them back in her pack?

"It's not the owl," she says. It's Darla's father. It's Sarah. It's the doll heads. It's time ticking away.

It's the owl. She shuts down, unplugs the laptop and stows it away. She changes into her new jeans and T-shirt and puts the sweatsuit in the Kmart bag, then in the suitcase. She puts on her tennis shoes and waits; she'll wait until the house falls silent for at least fifteen minutes. The owl calls a few times more, but Gretta feels more than ready to leave. She reaches in her pack and grasps the bandana-covered whistle until her fear subsides.

She rips a map out of a tabloid-thin phonebook and studies it. She had been on the right road all along, as far as she can tell. She only thought she was lost. She writes a thank-you note on the back of a receipt with a grape-scented Hello Kitty pen and leaves the note on the bed. She writes another note on the back of a graded spelling quiz: *Don't forget to write! smokingwaffle@yahoo.com.* She folds up the paper and tucks it into one of Darla's shoes. She tiptoes out of the room, her arms full, and trips on nothing; she recovers herself and resists an urge to take one last look at the mounted doll heads.

Outside, she sees no owl. *Of course you don't—it's dark.* She crams her stuff into the backseat. The engine turns over in only three tries, as a fairy might grant wishes. She considers this an omen of good things to come, upstaging even the owl.

Fruit Sauce Should Always Be Served on the Side

THE CAFÉ is dirty. There are cloth napkins on the tables on this side of the room. They have red stains and the ashtrays haven't been changed. Gretta speculates that it's because this is a bar-café. Drunks care less about cleanliness.

Not true. You've had quite a bit of gin, and I'm disgusted.

"What time do you close?" she asked when she walked in.

"Technically, about one. Maybe one-fifteen, one-thirty. But we're not going to kick you out or anything," said an old man swiveling on a barstool.

"Don't listen to Ben," the bartender said, glaring at the old guy. "He don't work here. We close at one o'clock."

Now, eighteen minutes later, it's a few minutes past one and her food hasn't yet been brought to her table. She finishes off a second gin-and-tonic from the bar—an indulgence, given that she's been working on a pint in her pack and the cough syrup alone had her rummy. She tries to calculate on a napkin whether she could be in Arizona by late morning.

By tomorrow afternoon—*at the latest!*—Gretta will have stuttered in front of one flea-market *Last Supper* tapestry, two oil paintings each of Manuelito and Barboncito, twenty-some family photos (she is not in them), two marriage baskets, and a sobering Aunt Angela. She will chew spearmint gum—a lot of it.

"Does anyone have a phone?" asks a man who has just rushed through the door. Gretta looks around. She can see the man's mistake. Outside the bar there are two signs: BAR on the left and CAFE on the right. Inside, it looks like one room. One room, one phone.

The bartender shakes his head no. Ben and a waitress pushing sixty do the same.

"Shit!" the guy says. He moans. "Come on, you've got to have a phone."

"Not one that works," says the bartender.

"God. God, god, god. Can I have a shot of tequila, please? With lime. I can't drink it without the lime."

The bartender nods, pushes a stepstool in place to reach a bottle of Cuervo.

"Good," the man says. "Good. I have some money." His hair is matted and fuzzy, something like a camel's, but his features are feminine. He looks like a crevice—a big, shady crevice. Gretta can picture him at the top of a building, feeling regretful. Or in a park, getting a rush. She could see him in a city, pretending to not be afraid of the darkening streets. *The air was cold as night—*

Gretta's throat is swollen and it's everything she can do to swallow. The man—the dense, graceful movement of his limbs—is a nice enough distraction, but still, gravity is getting to her. He notices her looking at him. He drinks the tequila.

As sweet as a rose was by sight.

She can't afford having Darla's sensibility edging in on her. The poem is stuck in her head nonetheless.

"Six-fifty," says the bartender.

The man takes money from his wallet, which looks to be full, and lays a bill on the bar. "Another," he says. He gestures the bartender close. He leans down as if to whisper into the bartender's ear and, falling short of the ear, mumbles indiscernibly, or is it that Gretta's brain fails to discern?

Somewhere there is a grassy clearing through which a clear stream courses. The smell of the wet brush and the grass is heady; it makes her dizzy. *This man—this fucking idiot—is nowhere near my stream.* She wonders who is or who could be. Either she needs another drink or she needed a few fewer: she is at a loss.

The bartender pounds his fist on the bar. "There's one phone around here, you little piss-ant, and it's in my kitchen, in my house, with my wife."

Piss-ant, the tequila man is not—he's possibly twice the size of the bartender—but he breaks a mutual stare with him by offering more money. With that, he drinks a second shot, and then a third.

The waitress brings Gretta fries, cheesecake, and gin. "Last call," she says, stretching one arm to the side and then the other.

"You sure all you've got is Beefeater?" It sounds to her almost pornographic, almost unbearable.

"Is that all?" the waitress says. She rolls her eyes then gathers bottles of ketchup and Heinz 57 from the five booths that make up the dining area.

"One more," says the man. "More lime." He looks at Gretta, who is staring at him. She turns away. Her mother has always complained about how she stares. She can't help herself. She has a penchant for staring. Like her penchant for sucking on rock candy. For the longest time, she believed no one could or would see her staring. To this day she forgets.

She wishes she had some rock candy. She wouldn't mind a map.

She tried to get out of feature writing and start a map-publishing business six years ago, but as she had no capital and couldn't make maps, she failed. She thought, *Hire someone.* But hiring someone was more difficult than she expected. For example, how can you tell a mapmaker from a mechanic if you don't know anything about either? She didn't hire a mechanic. She hired a graphic artist who specialized in drawing auto parts and land-reclamation equipment on Macintoshes. He didn't know anything about geography, he told her finally.

So Lance and Gretta went to the university library twice a week. One way or another, Lance said, they would make the business happen for her, even if he had to haul it home in a wheelbarrow. "Never give up on your dreams!" and "Follow your heart!" and "Dreams can come true!" he'd say. He became fascinated with cartography, so when Gretta wasn't, she had to beg him to give up on her.

She decided to collect rocks. She had bought the crystals book, that ode to the universe with a capital U, but by way of a return to the library, she found herself engaged in a semblance of geology. She had high ambitions, but unfortunately, she got lost on her first rock-hounding expedition. She didn't have food or matches or toilet paper or tampons. *One day I'll learn how to light a fire Boy Scout style,* she thinks. *I'll know how to make a Bunsen burner.*

She confuses herself. She starts off with one idea, ends up in another, forgetting where she came from or where she's going. She is not sure whether it's the Zoloft or the gin, or the Zoloft with gin, or the lack of orgasms thereof.

The French fries are soggy. The cheesecake is tolerable, minus the strawberry sauce. She sees the table in front of her has crackers. She snatches them quickly when the bartender turns to stock glasses.

After stuffing her pack with crackers, she waves the waitress back to her table. "Fruit sauce should always be served on the side." When she asks for the check, the waitress walks away without response. Gretta leaves a twenty under the plate. The bartender's head is off-center with suspicion as he watches her walk out the door, making her feel like she's swaggering, with one heavy fucking leg.

The tequila man is outside on the step, just beyond the illumination of the lamp over the door. "Hey, where you going?" he says.

Exactly what I said, she thinks, suddenly remembering what Lance said to her the last time she saw him. She recalls also the exact features of his expressionless face.

"Hey, where are you going?" she asked.

"The store," Lance answered, slamming the door shut. That was four and a half months ago, but by that time, Gretta understood the tone of his voice to mean *a very long time*. A few days, a few weeks—who knew. When a few months passed, she got the picture.

"South. Interested?" she says to the tequila man. He follows her, his hands jammed in his pockets. "You want to drive?" she asks. He shakes his head no. "Just a second," Gretta says once they step into the truck, but he has already begun to settle in against the door for a nap.

"I have to check my messages. You sure you don't want to drive? I'm not in great shape, I have to tell you."

"I'm sure," he says.

Bill: "Why do the burgers have to be Pakistani? Is this you making trouble again? Let's talk." *Right again.* Next time she'll do All-American Burgers, just to be fair. *Musharraf will understand.*

Renee: "Gretta! This is Lance's mother…." Gretta snaps her phone shut.

"That doesn't sound good," the tequila man says.

"Yeah, my boss is an asshole. My mother-in-law—she doesn't like me very much."

"Hello. I didn't hear your messages. I'm talking about your truck—you'd better get this thing in."

She gives the ignition a few more tries, slaps the steering wheel with both hands, and delivers a string of obscenities. "Maybe you should drive, seriously," she says, and just as quickly sees herself turning the key, saying, *Maybe you should drive, seriously.* She is being watched. The woman is either behind her or on the other side of the glass. Gretta begins to sink, begins to burn. Begins to feel sick—really sick.

The tequila man tries in vain to open the passenger window, then stops and leans close to Gretta. She sees that his skin is pale and entirely without wrinkles, but ruddy, and his nose is runny. The woman is frustrated—not so much with the runny-nosed rider, who seems irrelevant to her, but with the driver, with Gretta.

"What's going on?" he asks.

The woman urges. She insists. "Nothing."

"Do you have asthma, or…"

Inhale two, three; exhale two, three, four…. She closes her eyes.

"Is this, like, a panic attack?"

Shut up, let it pass. Shut up, let it pass. Gretta doesn't dare look back at the tequila man or at the woman. *Exhale two, three…* "Go away."

He starts to get out of the truck. She grabs his wrist and leans into the steering wheel.

"Not you! Talk to me. Talk about anything."

"Like…do you need an ambulance? A puffer? Do you need to lay down?"

"It'll go away. Where were you born?"

"Okay, this is…are you okay?"

"Just. Tell me. Make it up, for fuck's sake."

"Okay. All right. There was this carnie, a real old guy. He was walking by the bathrooms late at night, and—you sure you're okay?"

"Talk!" *Inhale two, three; exhale two, three, four…*

"And…they were closing up the place. And he heard my mom kind of screaming. And he went for help, so there was this…balloon guy and a janitor. Oh, and the candy-corn lady who went after some towels. This is strange."

"Fuck, fuck, fuck, fuck…," Gretta hears herself whisper.

"So but first my mom yells, 'I don't need towels; I need a fucking ambulance.' So the lady runs off crying and, I guess, makes the call. Balloon guy is all pissed off—*Where is your husband?* he wants to know. *Where is your father?* Like that. Janitor just keeps crossing himself and praying, real nice, like. Is this okay? Is this all right?"

"Yes."

"So janitor is holding her hand…. You look—feeling better yet?"

"Yeah, it's going away now. Just keep talking, please. Thanks."

"Balloon guy goes back to his balloons. Candy-corn lady…I don't know what happened to her." He waits. "What the hell was that?"

"Did she make it to the ambulance before you were born?"

"No. I mean, I was going to tell you no so I could drag it out, but yes. I was born at Saint Francis's General Hospital. Janitor came along. Uncle Sammy, I call him now. Nice guy. You know, I don't think you should drive."

"That's what I tried to tell you." She tries to smile. Now that he likely suspects she's crazy, she doesn't want him driving her pickup—not while she's sleeping. Who knows where she'd wake up. "I'm all right now. See? She's gone."

"Who's gone?"

"It's gone, I said." She tries the ignition again; eventually, the engine turns over.

"Still don't look so good."

"Just a little nauseous. It's seizures. I'm not crazy or anything, if that's what you're thinking."

"Yeah, okay. I mean, you didn't flop around or nothing."

"These are not those. They come and go. Thirty seconds. Two minutes, max. Like a long déjà vu. You've had déjà vu, haven't you? I'm all right. See? Nothing now."

"Here," he says, getting into his backpack. He pulls out a CD. "You want to listen to this? Puddle of Mudd—their newest one…."

"No CD player," Gretta says, nodding toward the stereo. "Tape deck."

"Wow. Okay, you got any tapes?"

"Indian music—recorded at powwows. Sound isn't too good."

"Let's hear it."

She points to the glovebox; he fishes around till he finds the tape. He reads the label: "Connecticut 1999."

"That's the one," says Gretta.

He puts the tape in. She waits for a reaction, a never mind. "Nice," he says. "Not quite what I expected, but I like it."

"Go ahead and sleep. I'll wake you up when we get to Moab."

The Curiously Multifaceted Nature of Victimization

"YOU'RE PATHETIC."

"I'm not pathetic."

"You're a real victim."

"I never said I was a victim." *Who is this person? And why did you let him in?*

The tequila man woke up less than a half-hour down the road, itching his feet as if to itch them off his legs. He was ornery but seemed hungry for conversation, asking her all kinds of questions. He seemed to be listening to her answers with some interest or she would have shut up. He nodded amiably, even threw in a few I-know-what-you-means. But now that he's given up on his feet and put his smelly hiking books back on, he looks at her scathingly.

"He's fucking around. His folks don't like you. You don't like your setup. *Move on.*"

"I didn't say I wasn't. I'm moving on. I'm moving—what makes you think you know what direction *on* is?"

"Next it'll be, 'Oh, but I love him!' Spare me the anguish and the human suffering, will you?"

Get rid of him. "You want a ride or not?"

"We're already on the road, if you haven't noticed. I'm just saying…pass me the bottle, please…and I'm only saying this because I like you…but stop being a dumbass. That's all I'm saying." He finishes the bottle. Fortunately, Gretta has another. "Mind if I have one of these?" He gestures toward Gretta's carton of cigarettes. She nods, expecting him to take a cigarette, but he takes a pack.

She wonders how unethical it would be to drop him off in a dark wasteland at the side of the road. *Unforgivable? Semiforgivable, given the circumstances?*

"Want some acid?" he says, his voice conciliatory.

"I have kids…seizures…." She looks at him carefully to see if he's joking. He holds a folded-up piece of foil out to her as if passing her a ring. She shakes her head. "You saw me falling apart. I can't take that stuff anymore."

"I have, like, eight hits. Plenty enough to go around."

"Can you not do that now? Can you put it away, please? If a cop pulls us over—"

"If a cop pulls us over, you're screwed. You're a goddamned…pickle or something."

"Thanks. You know, you keep doing that shit and you'll be as fucked up as I am. That's what my neurologist says."

"That I'll be as fucked up as you are?"

"No. The acid. It fucked me up. Brain damage or something."

"Or so he says. How would he know?"

"I mean, he said it was possible."

"So it's *possible* I will be as fucked up as you are." He laughs, shakes his dark curly mop out of his eyes. "How do you know I'm not now? Fucked up. As you are."

Gretta feels defensive. *You think I'm fucked up, then?* But she remembers the tequila man was not the one who made the characterization.

"You know," he says, "some people won't call a pickle a pickle unless it bounces three inches when thrown on the ground." He appears serious. "Or is it six inches? Seven? Eight? I don't know, but it's got to bounce, I know that. I'm just going to put two hits right here in case you change your mind. Look, see? That's what a nice guy I am. I'm going to fold yours up in this here gum wrapper…want the gum? No? From mi casa to…you casa. You don't want them, sell them. How's that?" He opens the ashtray. "I guess that's not…you're really messy, anyone ever tell you that? All right, the glove box, then."

"Did you just take that? Did you already take a hit?"

He sticks his tongue in and out, displaying a tiny square of paper. He stares at her a while, says, "Why are you so uptight?"

"Why are *you* so uptight? I mean, you came into the bar—"

"Check it out," he says. He lifts his shirt up. His side shows the first signs of a serious bruise. A four-inch cut from his left nipple south is clotted with blood. "He just scraped the top of it. Guy I was riding with. He thought I had money. I don't, you know. So don't even ask."

Gretta takes a new bottle of gin from under her seat and passes it to him. "I wonder why he'd think something like that." She mocks, "'Look, I have some money, see all my money.'"

He smiles at her for the first time since leaving the bar. It's a nice smile—effusive, toothy, possibly genuine. "You know how to take it, right? You keep it under your tongue, right here—"

"I *know* how to take it. I just can't, that's all."

He leans forward and watches her until she fidgets nervously with Sagittarius, who hangs from the ignition. "Want to have sex?" he asks.

She stares at him a moment too long and swerves onto the shoulder.

"I thought I was pathetic."

"You are. Who isn't?"

"Who are you? I mean, what's your name?"

"Wellington, five miles," he reads.

She considers possibilities, probabilities, obligations. *Five miles. Moab 5. Wellington 5. High five.* Is it regulation to warn of every town exactly five miles beforehand? *Does syphilis still exist?* Does James think about her at night, and if he does, does he dispel the thoughts into a sock marked Bitsilly? *And if syphilis still exists, does it really make your nose fall off?*

Lance *is* likely fucking around. She wonders how long it's been going on. With how many people. In what exact way. *Does it matter? He left you.* She has no moral standing to defend. *Do I?* She pulls over, puts the pickup in Park, and sets the emergency brake. "Okay. Let's go."

"What?"

She stretches her spine, which is tight from the drive. "You want to fuck or not? But you're not happy until I'm happy. Know what I mean?"

"Well, hell." He gingerly touches the wound over his shirt. "Stop in Wellington? Get a room? I'll buy."

Pathetic victims are left for dead in motel rooms. *Pathetic victims even fall in love in hotel rooms.* "I might change my mind by Wellington," she says.

He grins, rubs the side of his nose in seeming slow motion.

"Do you have a condom?" she asks.

"Sure." He waits. "You going to turn the ignition off?"

"No."

"At least turn off your headlights. We don't want to attract attention."

When she takes off her shirt, he stops her. "You're not going to have one of those things, are you? Like, one of those freaky déjà vus?"

"No. You scared?"

"No."

He smells of apples and garlic, tobacco and tequila. His hands are rough as plywood. He leans over and tries to kiss her, but she turns her head, so he kisses her neck instead—a little sloppy, but warm and evocative. When Gretta lies back on the seat, she finds herself sucking her stomach in and straightening her spine in what she considers a shameful attempt to impress him. He tries to move on top without squishing her. He unbuttons his pants, scoots them off his legs awkwardly, and kisses her belly and the larger of her two breasts on his way up.

"You happy yet?" he asks. He unbuttons his shirt, tosses it aside.

"Oh, no, that's not what I meant," she says, pushing down lightly on his shoulders, a suggestion. His grin is contagious.

The movements are awkward and contortionistic and the nudity inspires thoughts of policemen, handcuffs. There's no room for the tequila man on the seat so he gets down on the pop-sticky floor on the passenger side. They form something of an L. His mouth is warm and his tongue is diligent. He clears his pharynx. Gretta laughs. He continues, but Gretta can't stop laughing. "Shut up," he tries to say, but, diligent as he is, his voice is muffled. She keeps giggling, but, with a degree of pity for him and concern about her own pharmaceutically stunted libido, concentrates.

Lance comes to mind. Hurt-feelings Lance. Betrayed and shaking-chin Lance. Just-came Lance. Lance professing his love and asking her to do the same. *And when she snuck out the window—*

Lance saying, "It figures." Lance peeking in at her, grateful she has found something to obsess about besides him. James, hit suddenly with shrapnel. *He's on a ship, Gretta.* James, watching Southeast Asian dancers perform amazing vaginal stunts before a smoky crowd of desperately horny if not openly masturbating and likely married squids. James, lost and sweaty and sucking in invisible swirls of depleted uranium in Iraq.

He held up a flashlight—

James, producing fingerless babies.

Her clitoris is feeling withdrawn, dead to the world. She worries for the tequila man's jaw. She doesn't like the guy, necessarily, but she has respect for the oral workout he must be undergoing. She buries images of Lance and his brother under layers of other, more explicitly sexual images. Unbearably soft breasts come to mind. Nipples with the traction of a rubber stamp. Lips, lips, and more voluminous lips. And—*Yes.... No, no! Yes*—amazing vaginal stunts. The closer she comes to the tequila man, the more he is displaced by an idea—a figment marked by, among other things, curvature and perfect alignment.

She grasps the handle above her, imagines her wrists are bound there. She understands that in so doing, she has entered The Romance—the narrative she hates most, the one where the woman is metaphorically or physically raped and she likes it. *The cad,* the protagonist thinks. Right before her breasts *swell* or *heave* or miraculously become both *creamy* and *firm* at the same time. Right before she falls in love and is left.

Concentrate. She thinks *fingers,* he responds. She thinks *faster,* he complies. She thinks—

No, no, no, no, no.... When she returns to the phallus, she feels ground, eaten. Divided into many. *Unass my AO, li'l soldier.* Her eyes tear. She wipes them inconspicuously because it is suddenly everything to her to not be pathetic. "Not yet! Almost."

She has locked herself in a genre but is determined to get out. Determined, but so very dizzy.

Concentrate: curvature, alignment, *white phosphorous? Concentrate:* love, clitoris. Duct tape.

The concentration of her cracks, rends, divides, reveals a collage of body parts, male and female alike—faceless, fragmented, overlapping—

—And Zoloft Almighty is defeated. She thanks god she hasn't started taking the Dilantin again or she might never have come.

The tequila man appears, ruddy-faced, between her legs. She holds up a trembling hand. *Wait a minute,* she means to say. He nods in acknowledgement, his face glistening. "Give me a sec," he says, rummaging through the pockets of his pants. He gets out of the truck, peeling open and smoothing on his protection. Gretta stretches her tight, shaking legs.

"Could you do me a favor first?" she says, humored by the scratch in her voice, something she hasn't heard in a long—*so very long*—time. "There's a towel in the bed of the truck. Get me the towel." When he does, she reaches for the door handle, slams the door shut, and locks it; she scoots to the driver's side and locks it as well. She drives forward, slowly at first, so as not to run over his feet or knock him over. He bangs on the side of the truck as she drives away. He yells. She opens her window and throws his clothes out on the road. She floors it—naked, delirious, saturated with a more palatable variety of romance, contemplating the curiously multifaceted nature of victimization.

The Wavering Red Light

GRETTA'S BREASTS and belly are blue in the light of the computer screen. The end of her cigarette, by contrast, lights up red. So very, very red.

TheLover.doc

It is 1996. It could be anytime in fall. I know this because I'm sneezing. Lance's pores are open. His eyelashes are long, his eyebrows wide and scattered. His forehead shines.

When he's being looked at, he can't look. To look is to feel curious, to be interested, to lower himself.

Eight bodies lie in the grass outside the lodge. The steam rising from their bodies can be seen through the inconstant light of the fire in the ash-and-coal-filled fire pit.

A man holds a running hose over his head and wipes his face. It is Lance, suddenly and inexplicably repositioned from our grassy bed. A red dot which is the burning end of a cigarette can be seen wavering. It is his mother's.

Soon I will be cold. I get up, wrap a sweaty towel around my shoulders, step into my sandals. I walk around to the driveway, to the front of the old house—the big house that eclipses the trailer house, the past that eclipses the present, the extreme poverty that eclipses relative poverty. The old Victorian bears traces of magnificence: twelve-foot-high ceilings, intricate crown molding, the masonry and woodwork of men. Now abandoned. Left for something smaller. An appreciating asset left for a depreciating one, something smaller. I appreciate to nothingness, step by rotting step. As if the worn wooden stairs of the porch were always such—sweet nothingness, containing nothing, nothing coming, nothing going, a thought, a precedent. No one stops me. I am followed by dogs.

The porch steps are rounded with wear, both from my husband's family and the family of the farmer who lived in it before them. Who, after running the house ragged, rented it to a family of Native Americans in exchange for long hours, subminimum wages, and an absence of insurance in an environment of broken backs, missing fingers, sleepless harvests.

The door is not locked. The lights do not work; there are no bulbs, there is no service, not anymore. I am in the kitchen. I have seen it in the light. To my left are white cupboards. The walls are bright aqua blue, or orange, or both. I can't remember which. Inside these walls, Lance's parents threw raucous all-Indian parties: broken windows, broken limbs, broken vows. Inside these walls, they found the drum, brought to them by a friend, and soon after chose the drum over the bottle. They sobered up, for good. The vows, unspoken, sealed shut again and they took a good look at the children.

Six footsteps across raised, torn linoleum, I bump into nothing. I reach out—the wall is cold and almost soft. I feel around for the doorway, my hand gets caught on a nail. I suck on it, drawing blood. The wallpaper peels.

Have the stairs always groaned so loudly? When Lance and his sister jumped from the middle of the stairs to a stack of pillows at the bottom, did they bump their heads on the threshold like other kids might? Did they laugh despite? The rail up the stairs stops halfway up.

There are sixteen stairs. At the top stair, Lance once held a shotgun inside his mouth. "Just like you the first time," he explained. "Except mine was loaded." It is this top stair, or the door looming above it, that awaits me. It is as if it always has, if only to send me running back outside. I am an intruder, after all. I can't seem to help but intrude.

I am reminded of something Lance had said, that I belonged nowhere, that I wasn't responsible for my displacement. No more, he said, than he was. An off-reservation, intertribal Indian, fallen in love with a white girl.

I feel the walls, the floors, I have seen them in the light. Dead flies and dirt crunch under my sandals. Chunks of wall are missing. I follow the wallness up, up toward the door. It terrifies me. There is a knob. It is cold and smooth in my hand.

"You know, the author of that book was a Communist," Lance told Gretta when she first began reading *The Lover* some years back. "That's what I heard."

"You know what I herd?" Gretta said, co-opting Lance's favorite joke.

"Sheep," he answered, always the good sport.

"She *was* a Communist. She left the party. And so what if she was?"

He shrugged. "She was a Nazi sympathizer too."

"She *slept with* a Nazi sympathizer. Or so it is rumored."

"So maybe she was a racist too."

"You sleep with me—does that make you white?" That's what she said, but in truth some of the condescension with which "the little white girl" in *The Lover* described her Chinese john and the Vietnamese in general made the book difficult to read, much less digest. Sometimes it seemed that the very structure of the narrative cast a furtive glance toward Vietnam. But that didn't mean she was inclined to back down. "Have you ever even read the book?" she could have asked, a wild card, but she thought of something better. She grinned unbearably because she knew she had him in a corner: "Better yet, *I* sleep with *you*. Does that make me Indian?"

An Unspeakable Shine

Thump, thump. That's how innocuous it can sound when you take a life. Gretta pulls to the side of the road, though the decision to turn around and shine her brights on it is slower in coming.

It's furry and it yowls.

She dresses finally, in the jeans and T-shirt wadded up on the floor. A smile and a horror emerge beyond the yowling when she envisions the tequila man searching through the near-moonless night, on acid, for his shirt, tossed on the highway.

She gropes under and behind the seat for something useful. A camera phone won't help. The shovel in the back of the pickup is in order if it dies, *but if it lives—?* She finds a banged-up ABBA tape—not hers, wouldn't be Lance's. New jumper cables. *How very thoughtful of him, knowing he would ditch you.* A Maverik mug with traces of chew in it. An Allen wrench. *Roast-beef string?* She is stumped but takes it anyway because it's the closest thing to useful she can find. Kmart bag, maybe. She stuffs one in her back pocket.

She pushes through the headlights and the gin. The thing growls. It yelps. Its eyes reflect the headlights with an unspeakable shine. Gretta never thought she would be lucky enough to see a real live fox—or a real dead fox—any fox that hasn't been stuffed and put on display or encased in glass in some lifelike—that is, some very unlifelike—scenario at the zoo. But it couldn't be anything else: gray on top, red on the bottom, white throat. It's a fox. A gray fox, maybe. Its back leg is mashed on the highway. The leg appears cauterized but still red and pulpy. The fox smells like birdseed, Wite-Out, and a bloody nose, and also strangely like cake batter. She drops the string and takes off her T-shirt, wondering if she will be bitten. If—*please God*—it could be fatal. She wedges the shovel under her arm, covers the fox with the T-shirt, and scoops him up. He is heavier than she expected, at least thirty pounds. The leg sticks. She wedges the top of the shovel under it, scrapes a bit. The leg releases like a worn rubber band. What's left of the leg dangles. The rest of it sticks to the asphalt. Gretta struggles not to gag, but considers all the same whether she ought to pull the paw off the road—*toss in his glower dart and bag it up for the vet.* She wonders how she can both hold the fox and work the shovel some more—

Don't be ridiculous. He'll have to walk on it. Run. Hunt. If the paw has bone left in it, it's now the consistency of rock salt. There will be no sewing back on of the paw.

The animal yowls and tries to wriggle away. Adrenaline shoots through her fingers with every miserable sound and movement, but by the time she reaches the truck, the thing goes limp and relatively quiet.

With the fox strapped ineffectively in the passenger seat, she drives toward Moab, or so she thinks until she sees a small sign, THOMPSON. She pulls into a gas station off the highway and asks the very large, very red clerk inside how close she is to Moab. He slaps a map on the counter and unfolds it, peering at her. She wonders if he can smell alcohol on her breath, if he will call the highway patrol. *You* are *a drunk driver.*

"You see the sign?"

"Yeah, Thompson. I just came from Green River. I'm trying to get to Moab."

"No shirt, no shoes, no service. Here, you take the map. I got dozens."

Ah! She looks down at her new bra—white, bloodstained, a bit padded. "It's a swimming suit," she says.

He shakes his head derisively in the manner of reality-TV characters. "I don't think I have to tell you you're going the wrong way. See, you was supposed to take this road about thirty miles down to Moab. Looks like you shot right past the turnoff and came up over here."

"Christ."

He sighs dramatically and shakes his head. Gretta looks for a hidden camera. Would she appear on some reality TV show looking like hell in a bloody bra?

"If you want to parade around here in your underwears this early in the morning, that's just fine, but I'd appreciate your not taking the lord's name in vain."

Didn't "the lord" refer to God, not Jesus? Or was it the other way around? *Oh, lord. House of Lords. A lordly demeanor. Your lordship. Lordy, lordy, lordy.* Nothing signifies specifically—not to her. She considers seizing the opportunity of clearing up the issue with someone who would know, but the clerk doesn't strike her as receptive to such a conversation.

Instead: "You got a hotel here?"

In the truck, she pours a shot of gin on the fox's hindquarters. He protests sharply, undermining the sense of generosity that comes with sharing a drink. He trembles. She wonders what she will do with the fox if she is able to find a vet and get it fixed. Would Fish and Game be called in? Could she take the animal home? Is there a law against leashing fox? Does Fish and Game carry equipment for testing blood-alcohol content? She considers these and other things, always coming round to the same basic question: Will Lance come home with her?

She wonders what he would think of this. He probably would think it makes sense—that there she is, toting around a dead wild or not-so-wild and not-exactly-dead animal. He'd probably know right what to do. He'd put the animal out of its misery, or he'd rig up a clever leg sling made of Popsicle sticks and tooth floss that would actually work. The fox would no doubt sense he was in good hands and calm down. That's how Lance is: good hands. *Not so, you.*

She wonders why the fox hasn't tried to bite her. *Maybe,* she tells herself, *you're not threatening enough.* Still, she has to wonder, does she no longer appear worth eating? *Idiot—foxes don't eat people.* She wants to stare and stare at her bit of nature, wrapped in a bloody T-shirt.

Twilight will soon give way to day. She is not ready. She rests her head on the steering wheel until a low, sad yowl propels her.

Entering the Third Dimension

GRETTA TOSSES a Visa card on the counter, struggling to keep the fox from slipping out of her arms. "You can't have dogs in here. It's a policy." The hotel clerk lifts his head and squints at her. He reminds Gretta of something. Something she doesn't like, she's not sure what. Maybe the last clerk.

Saveloy, she imagines herself saying. *That's a ready-cooked, highly seasoned dry sausage to you. Pig's brains!* She wonders why he assumes the bloody mass in her arms is alive. Only his head is visible outside the T-shirt, and a pale delicate tongue hangs comically to the side of his muzzle. "The *dog* will be sleeping in my vehicle," she tells the clerk. "Is there a vet around here?"

He laughs. She looks around his office for an insult. Little dirty cash register. Halogen lamp on a big, white wooden desk. Case of Dr. Pepper in the corner, on top of a beat-up, gummy filing cabinet, a stack of newspapers, and FedEx envelopes. There is too much or too little to say, and she is so very tired.

"Check-in time isn't till three."

"So charge me for last night. I need a bed now." If she fails to wake up, she reminds herself, she won't have to pay anything.

"All right, then. Checkout time *tomorrow* is ten-thirty." He runs the card, offers her a Visa slip to sign. "You look familiar," he says.

"I'm not from around here."

"I got it—I saw you at Ray's the other night. Monday? Tuesday? You were playing pool."

"Ray's Tavern?" Ray's is one of her favorite stops along the way to the reservation—it has been for years. *The fork photo, maybe?* "Was I with anyone?"

He shrugs.

"Come on, was I with anyone?"

"I don't know, were you?" he says sarcastically. He looks her up and down as if he has earned the right to, as if he knows something scandalous.

"I was on my way to Moab."

"And now?"

"I'm on my way to Moab again."

"You traveling on business?"

"You got to know?"

He shakes his head, holds his hands up.

Hold your fire! Hold your fire, goddamn it! What would it take, she wonders, to feel less compelled to be mean? To be within a more normal range of passive aggressiveness? Fewer war movies? A new drug? More therapy?

She passes the signed slip back. "Pleasure. I only travel on pleasure."

A good night's sleep? "Twelve little steps," Lance would say.

The fact is, she tried the Twelve Steps. She had problems with steps one and two, which seemed at the time to resonate with some forms of fascism, but got entirely hung up on step three: *Made a decision to turn our will and our lives over to the care of God as we understood Him.* No sponsor seemed supportive of having her skip it. ("Go ahead and try to skip step three…you'll run into steps five, six, seven, eleven. You can't escape God, Gretta.") She wasn't about to turn her will and life over to anything—if she chose life, she would need will, she was convinced. And turn them over to God? If she could believe in God, she probably would. But not to any "him," certainly not to Him capitalized. It pissed her off. "You don't have to see God as male," her first sponsor in a series of four explained. "Just…a higher power, you know. It could be anything that comes to mind." The old man with a beard and a staff clearly won't do it for her. Flowy, fairy mother goddesses won't do it either. Every avenue seems to lead to Hollywood, the Bible, or at the very least to Joseph Campbell, and she's left feeling like a befuddled wanna-be something, when all she really wants to be is at peace. With what, she isn't apt to define, specifically.

She tried to come up with a suitable image for a higher power, but every time she and Lance would show up for a meeting at Fellowship Hall, a toothless biker or repentant bricklayer would say, "My god is an Indian on a white horse" or something like it, then look at Lance meaningfully. Gretta wanted nothing more than to crawl under the table—either embarrassed for being white or bothered by the sheer sentimentality of the gaze. Now when she tries to come up with a less archetypal candidate for a higher power—a flying turtle, a wispy cloud, a magical sparkling ball of dust—she wonders just how asinine it is in, surely, somebody's eyes. ("I wanted to believe, but some failed writer came to the meeting today, claiming a unicyclist sloth as her higher power.") And to what end? Nancy Albertson as in Albertsons is giving belief her best, and she doesn't seem at peace.

If peace is out of the question, then coma. Death. *Is it so much to ask?*

She settles in, cranking up the heat and rolling the blinds closed. She finds a Do Not Disturb sign on the nightstand and hangs it on the door outside, then locks the door. She situates the fox, takes a seat at something similar to a desk.

She feels like she should do something. She opens the makeshift drawer attached to the underside of a half of an old kitchen table. Inside she finds a phone book, hotel stationery, a well-worn Gideon's Bible—*Now, the doctor came in, stinking of gin*—and two pens, one reading Beehive Community Credit Union: Where Members Count, the other Reed's Auto Body and Repair Shop. The stationery is decent stock, if printed badly and bound on a cheap pad. One of the pens works (Reed's) with some tapping. She lies on the bed with the pen uplifted and the stationery pad propped up on the thin phone book. Nothing.

Then:

~ Two Rapids Hotel ~

Fun for the whole famly!

Divorce is like 3–D mapmaker's glasses. Suddenly you look at the world as if you were really there.

Then: nothing.

Two trips to the pickup and all of her stuff is in the room. She boots up, searches her files for the Twelve Steps. She starts with the first two.

Twelve.doc

1.) ~~We admitted we were powerless over alcohol—that our lives had become unmanageable.~~ I concede that I have long entertained the power of alcohol to console myself over the fact that life is by nature unmanageable.

2.) ~~Came to believe that a Power greater than ourselves could restore us to sanity.~~ Am coming to believe that this power of alcohol is not enough to restore me to sanity—or, alternatively, to suspend my concern about my sanity, or that rhetorical category, sanity.

A *Power* greater than ourselves. It seems to Gretta that most forms of authority rely on this premise. The power of the economy, of the nation-state, of the will of the people, of Chairman Mao, of George W., of advertising, of synergy (her boss's favorite word), of military might, Heil Hitler, Praise God. Praise Allah, Praise Adonai. All require an investment, all claim the ability to restore, none are transparent but all rely on the perception of transparency.

Hell, she can come up with any number of reasons to resist the original steps, yet somehow her rewrite doesn't seem any more palatable than AA's steps, much less capable of inspiring sobriety. It's possible that sobriety isn't something that's *inspired*, it just *transpires*. No one needs twelve steps to exercise. Rather, Jane Doe wakes up one day and takes a run rather than thinking about taking a run. The next day, she does it again, and so on. Or maybe she gives a gym sixty dollars then feels obliged to get her money's worth. Maybe the whole point is to feel invested in one's own sacrifice or struggle.

She closes her eyes and runs her hand across the balls of nylon that make up the bedspread. The pillow smells like her grandma's favorite chair—Pall Mall with a touch of lavender. That's what Gretta likes about cigarettes. They prove everything: in the lungs, burn; out, smoke. They leave traces of having been there. She wishes that were a standard for all of the many elements of life. She unwraps two of four plastic cups, breaks open a fifth of Gilbey's, pours herself a couple of drinks, and lights a cigarette. Just how much gin would it take to render a 138-pound girl impenetrable? Just what sort of trace might she leave on the pillows, in the walls? She considers the possibility that ghosts are real, that she herself would become a ghost trapped in a half-star motel. She and the fox would be obliged to attend prostitutes, escape artists on the move, and the loneliest of the lonely, truck drivers. Maybe she could rescue a few girls—whisper Oedipal conflicts into the ears of abusers, electrify the TV with reruns of *Touched by an Angel* at precisely the right moment to deflate sexual prowess. She could train the fox to gnaw on perpetrators' toes.

Alas…, she is needed elsewhere. Ghosts of her kids are with her—needing clothes, generating doctor bills, wondering about their role in their dad's disappearance. Tulip has needed a baton for dance at the Y for two months. *Couldn't even buy her a fucking baton, could you?* It's true, she sent her daughter to class with an aluminum chair leg. She pours a couple more drinks.

"September 8—Virgo. Grandma says that means I'm logical. Are you logical, too, Mom?" Maroon carpet beneath her black boots. Where is she? *Yes,* Tulip's first day of kindergarten. Gretta has managed twin zigzagged French braids for her daughter. She has equipped her with the best of clothes (though she cannot remember now what the clothes looked like) and a new *Nemo* bookbag half her size, all in hope that Tulip won't ever have to comprehend what it is to be ostracized.

Her mother's ghost is there too, asking her how she managed to get only four and a half hours down the highway in all this time—*how much time?* Lance stands in the doorway, wanting to be somewhere else—singing a song, on the phone making plans "for that powwow highway." And legal services, they're in the corner, telling her to document everything; she pours them a couple of drinks as well. Then there's work. The laptop grins from the desk-table, where it is juicing up for greater deeds. *Come on, I'll bounce you on my lap.*

She makes it to the bathroom before throwing up, then lies on the cool linoleum floor. She breathes deeply, with intention, and makes her way back to the bed. "I am here. There is just this room. There is just this bed…and this lamp and this desk and this shitty TV."

Don't forget the fox.

"Yes, the fox. The fox, the fox…."

She dreams of foxes in forests, foxes in jungles with swamps that suck the feet off the animals. She dreams of running through trees with no feet and no compass, dragging a burning fox through mud, dunking her arms in the mud to remove gummy napalm from her hands, losing both the fox and her hands.

When she wakes sometime later, hot-cold-hot-cold, curled up around *Desert Solitaire, Dispatches,* an empty fifth, and a near-empty bottle of Zoloft, she is neither a ghost nor in a coma nor smoking with napalm. The room is filled with the heavy scent of game and death. She checks the fox—he is still breathing, if erratically, but has pissed himself and the bed, making his scent all the more repugnant. She checks the time—11:47 P.M.

She phones the front desk, grateful for having hands with which to push buttons. "How much do I owe so far?"

"Give me a sec. Seventy-eight dollars plus tax, not including any long distance calls you may have made or pay-per-view movies you may have watched."

"You have pay-per-view movies?"

"We have a few."

"Like what?"

"Adult movies. You want one?"

Seventy-eight dollars. She is relieved—she must have checked in yesterday morning, which means it's only Friday.

"Hello?"

Friday! Jackie had a date on Friday. *Inhale two, three....* Calling to apologize is out of the question. *Sorry, Jackie...tried to drink myself to death. Didn't think you'd mind.* What *had* she been thinking? *Exhale two, three, four....* There's nothing she can do to fix it; she's several hours away from home. *Inhale two, three....* The date would have been over by now. *Exhale two, three, four....* She can say she was stranded... she can say she was kidnapped.... *Jackie's your friend....* She counts backward from thirty but calms down by eight.

She wishes Lance were here. He would insist on fresh sheets. He would complain that the room was too cold for his wife. "Happy anniversary," he'd say to her once they were comfortable. *Or was it yesterday? Day before? Tomorrow?* Or he would scowl about the gin on her breath, which he would surely smell, fox or no fox, gum or no gum. They would each lie unnaturally close to opposite edges of the bed, looking outward, pretending to sleep. Then again, she would have drunk less, or not at all, had they been together.

She could, however, have sent him after her meds, and she could have taken them all.

Don't be stupid. If she'd been serious about suicide, she would have paid for the room in cash. *You still would have been identified by license plates, your wallet, your laptop.* She couldn't stand the thought of being identified. Better her kids think of her as lost than as dead. Better they feel at loss than abandoned.

It's possible Jackie has already tried to find her. She checks her phone—it's out of battery. What would Lance do with the kids if they were left to him? What would he tell them about her as their memories faded? She returns to the bathroom and makes herself vomit. He would certainly be angry with her. He could say anything to them. "Nice anniversary present, eh, kids? Now do you see?"

"Happy anniversary to you too, darling," she says to the toilet. "Thanks for nine beautiful years."

On their second anniversary, Lance decided the two of them should have a second honeymoon. He'd gotten into the powwow scene and Gretta had started a new job putting together features for the Website end of an events publication, *The Wasatch Front.* At first Gretta tried to integrate powwows and work so she could spend more time with Lance. She'd put together photo essays of the powwow scene. She wanted to portray the people she saw every weekend not as the stoic environmentalists and spiritualists in mountain-man garb that she saw on the screen, but as the people who dumbfounded her most. That is, people who could make jokes to keep one another laughing all day long despite having to eat bologna or potato-chip sandwiches and sleep on a friend-of-a-friend's floor with a dozen other friends-of-said-friend, just to be able to make it to the powwow, spend time together, dance or watch each other dance. People who could pull into the camping area in a 1980s van yet be more than happy to put up a generous giveaway for a niece being sent off to college. Children dancing and running around together until one or two in the morning, happy as clams, then up again by nine to do it again. Singers with various day jobs—roofers, computer programmers, homemakers, cashiers, attorneys, the unemployed—all sitting around the drum together, equals, talking or practicing songs, wadding up greasy paper plates and throwing them at some unsuspecting friend or relative, then laughing their asses off. These were the images she wanted to take with her outside of the arena. But most of the dancers and singers were fed up with white people snapping shutters in their faces without so much as a pretty-please, so they were categorically fed up with her too. If her lens caught the eye of a dancer who caught the I of the lens, god forbid: "Got twenty dollars? Give me twenty dollars and yeah, you can take a picture of me. If not, you got no business pointing that thing at me."

When the powwow community found out she was married to Lance—that Lance had married *her*—it was worse. Some made sure she knew it. "What do you think you're doing?" they would ask him. The question needed no further explanation; Lance knew exactly what they meant. He ignored them, even told a couple of people to back off, but it didn't make it any easier for Gretta to sit in a lawn chair or on the bleachers with a heavy zoom lens, feeling the scorn. Today the thought of shooting a photo of a full-blooded Indian makes her nauseous.

"I'll sit this one out," she found herself saying here and there, then always. She'd help Lance make sure his ribbons were sealed at the ends with a lighter and the ketchup stains were removed from his regalia. On a good day, she'd kiss him and wave good-bye. On a bad day, she was angry for being left without a more persuasive invitation and he knew it. He'd remind her whose choice it was to stay home and sulk.

Both knew the marriage was slipping, though they rarely talked about it. So on the weekend of their second anniversary, Lance came home early. He'd driven all the way to Montana for a powwow and turned right around. "Let's just go away," he said. "Let's go somewhere nice, just you and me. Let's take that second honeymoon." Gretta was thrilled, but they were broke. That night, they got a hotel a couple hours out of town at a hot springs but returned home in the morning, their credit card declined on the second night. By the time they walked through the door of their apartment building, she had an idea: she would write to *The New Newlywed Game* and ask for an application.

The two were invited in for a screening. They didn't have enough money to make the trip, but they were able to catch a ride from friends who were going to L.A. to visit family.

Gretta and Lance weren't screened by the host. They were screened along with three other couples by a woman with red tights. Put into a studio with the other couples, they did well—at first. His favorite team was Pittsburgh, though she couldn't say which sport. The best present she ever got was an enlarger. His favorite food was macaroni salad. She liked whoopee two to three times per week.

"This question is for Gretta. 'What goes bump in the night? What is Lance most afraid of?'"

"Mice. If manipulated, they have the ability to—" Lance aimed an elbow at her side but instead the elbow rebounded off a chair arm and he cursed in pain. "Can I have another question?" Gretta asked.

"Fill in the blank: 'My husband is so funny, he had me in stitches when. . . .'"

Lance always made her laugh in the beginning, but suddenly it was unclear whether she had been laughing with him or without him, or what for. They had been stuck in their seriousness for a long time before the interview.

"It was when he pointed to his mom who had a little red coat on her back. 'Check out Mighty Mouse!' he said. 'She looks like Mighty Mouse!' I'd been trying hard to stay awake all night, trying to concentrate on the drum and not throw up the medicine—"

"You can't talk about that. Jesus!"

One of the couples stifled a laugh. "Let's move on," said the red-tighted woman.

"Give us one more chance. I'll be better, I promise," Gretta begged. She knew Lance wouldn't speak to her after the interview—that she'd blown any possibility for a second honeymoon.

"Lance, your wife is standing in line, waiting to shake hands with the president. Someone jumps in line in front of her. What does she say?"

He smiled, smug, despairing. "'Hey, jackass, I paid for this spot.'"

She was right. Lance didn't speak to her or touch her for a week.

The fox, she would like to believe, is still breathing—slowly. She checks her phone for messages. Nothing. She wishes she could sleep, but her mind is running circles around her exhausted body. She watches TV with the sense she is masturbating *sans* clitoris: A middle-aged Christian with eyes slapped in blue and glitter on her cheeks. A young man saying, "You too can become an overnight success." A young woman describing the latest carrot-peeling technology, at only three easy payments of $7.99 each, plus shipping and handling. "Adult movies" seem oddly appealing by comparison. *But a libido is the last thing you need.* She wonders how it would feel to fry naked at night in the desert, how long it would take to find one's feet.

She looks at her bloody shirt, still wrapped around the fox in the middle of the bed. She doesn't know what to do with it. *How long till a dead body starts to stink? How long till it gets hard?* She pokes it. It's soft and mushy. She'd like to think warm, but really it isn't much warmer than room temperature.

So pour yourself a tall one and have a seat.

She covers all but the fox's muzzle with the side of the bedspread, just in case, and runs herself a bath.

Forward, Anywhere

THEY SAY if you die in your dreams, you die in real life. Gretta wakes from a dream that she was murdered by Ronald McDonald. She remembers thinking in the dream, *This must be Armageddon.* Rain, deserts. Weird landscapes. Nuclear mushrooms. Ronald, who was deceiving a small crowd with cheap tricks, could make himself as tall as King Kong or as short as eleven feet so as to fit, hunched over, through the threshold of her apartment building. Her focus became clear; she moved, the whole of her, in one direction: forward, anywhere. In the end, he got her with a long metal rod that had a barbed hook on the tip of it.

She lies in the starchy bed for a while. She is alive—sick, cold, wondering what to do. The room stinks something awful. She gets up and throws her dirty clothes, a half-pack of cigarettes, and deodorant in her suitcase. When she finds the map, she finds also that it is stained with vomit. *Gah.* The taste in her mouth—she needs a toothbrush immediately. She considers washing off the map. *Fuck it,* she thinks. *If I get lost, it'll be fate. It'll be out of my hands.*

She showers, scrubs her teeth with a washrag, squeezes her aching temples with her palms. She considers crying, but she hasn't got the time. Now that the fox is undeniably dead and she has survived nearly a fifth of gin, a handful of Zoloft, and Ronald's rod, she resolves to confront Lance with a choice and get back to her children by midnight. She'll be home, unpacked, bathed, and ready to go to work by Monday.

On second thought, she takes the map. She wipes it off with a stiff white towel, stashes the rest of the plastic cups and the stationery into her pack.

She wants to pat the fox, give it a good-bye. She can't bring herself to make contact with such warmlessness. She tosses the room key next to the animal and leaves the door open.

Her pack and suitcase land in the bed of the truck with a crack. She stows the laptop beneath the seat. The air is still and silky from aridity. The sun is bright and somewhat warm, but she's cold nevertheless. The ignition clicks impotently. She rests her head on the steering wheel, her hands ten and two, and waits for some good luck.

Once, when her father took her family to church for the first and last time, she was left behind. A car wreck had convinced him to get religion. Her mother suggested they try Mormonism so as to fit into the community better, but Mormon families had too often sent Gretta (in tears) and her brother (cursing) home for not being members of the church.

"They can go straight to hell," her dad always said. So he took them to Christ's Church in Salt Lake. The pastor or minister or whatever he was—Gretta still doesn't know the difference—used Biblical quotes to call upon God to smite the sinners who danced and drank and coveted and took pleasure in mischief. Gretta's father was so angry, he ushered his family out of the pew and out of the building ("Wait! Let me get my coat!") and sped right out of the church parking lot—without her.

After the services, people filed out the front door and around her as she sat on the steps. The parking lot emptied. She cried. She tried to go back in. The door was locked. She wet her pants. She sat on the snow-packed, yellowed porch. A janitor appeared behind the glass, unlocked the front door to leave, and locked the door behind him. He asked her if she was okay. She said she was. Her father would come back for her. And he did, almost three hours later, just before dark; her toes felt ringed by ice and her fingers were long since numb.

"We thought you were in the backseat," her mother explained. "Your brother didn't say a thing. And your father—well, I'm sorry,

Gretchen—we've all had a lot on our minds."

She tries the ignition again. It works, with some reluctance. She is one step closer to her destination.

Maybe she's not ready. *What'll you say?*

"Lance, your children need you." They do miss him. They misbehave in honor of their loss. "Lance, I need you."

No, no, and fuck no.

~ Two Rapids Hotel ~

Fun for the whole famly!

> *Resolve: DISSOLVE, MELT; BREAK UP, SEPARATE <the prism resolved the light into a play of color>; also: to change by disintegration, to reduce by analysis. To cause resolution of (a pathological state). To deal with successfully: clear up. To reach a firm decision. . .intrans. CONSULT, DELIBERATE. . .to progress from dissonance to consonance.*

She is not convinced of the existence of consonance, except perhaps in music. That, in her mind, reveals the dream of music for what it is: hope.

> *Responsibility: The quality or state of being responsible: as moral, legal, or mental accountability.*

She flips through the dictionary for something more persuasive but feels overcome with something closer to predilection.

> *Futility: The quality or state of being futile: USELESSNESS. A useless act or gesture <The futilities of debate for its own sake —W.A. White>*

Futile as her push south seems to be, Gretta can't very well keep turning around. If she drives back home now, she might be back later with less money for gas. Her children, she decides, will not spend their adulthood getting confessional in Al-Anon or AA. They will not be motherless and they will not be fatherless, in spirit or otherwise. *Or at least they will not be motherless.* They will go to college, if she has anything to say about it. They will travel. They will accompany her to therapy and develop vast amounts of self-esteem. They will see much more of their mother in the future, if she has to stay home and spin freakish doll-head doilies to earn a living. Gretta will force her relationship with Lance to some conclusion so she can get on with, at the very least, a parenthood strategy, because there can't be anything futile in that. Her sobriety would not require a drum, but a commitment—to her kids, to herself. To the possibility of "looking upon beauty," as Lance's father would say, without feeling loss and regret.

If she had to start up a new AA, she would—Agnostic Alcoholics, maybe. She could be her only member so as not to fear her impact on the unwitting. She'd continue her rewrite of the Twelve Steps, then she would follow them. *Jane Doe wakes up one day and takes a run rather than thinking about taking a run. The next day, she does it again.* There it is: a resolution.

What Becomes of Virginia Dare

M.Butterfly.doc

```
G: I have a vision. Of Roanoke. That, deep within its almond eyes, there is curiosity: Croatoans willing to extend mercy to a scrawny white baby girl for the art of seeing what happens next. Even an infant whose life is completely without worth.

G: I have a vision. Of Native America. That, deep within its almond eyes, there is a battle waiting to be won. There is a resolve that would cut the throat of a white baby girl if it would let the blood out of an empire blistering the continent with corruption, with violence, with greed.
```

These competing visions of the world are not so much her own as they are flat, colored stones along a riverbank, which she casts into a tributary of the Colorado River, watching them skip across the surface four, maybe five or six times.

Nineteen calls from Jackie and seven from her mother on her Recent Calls list. NO MESSAGES. The silence is the part that scares her most. The silence keeps her from returning the phone calls.

In the Vat Lies the Fruit

PERHAPS FOR *resolve*—dissolve/separate/melt/deliberate/decide/reduce—the dictionary is fixed on no particular order.

Gretta got out of the truck. She has followed an arrow drawn on a paper plate that was stuck to a fence at the side of the road. It pointed to a fairly smooth gravel trail. She found at the end of the road not a family picnic, not a rancher's yard sale, but another, smaller trail, another sign, engraved in wood: ANASAZI RUINS.

From the road all she could see was sagebrush, juniper, rust-colored buttes in the distance. But a little over fifteen minutes south and the path took a sudden turn for beauty, passing without warning into a small canyon. On the whole, it's blue and gold and red and rocky. It's curvy and terribly rigid, not so different from the San Rafael Swell. Not so similar that it stops her from getting choked up, which pisses her off considerably.

She descends a few feet down the path and touches the face of a rock carved subtly, perfectly, by, she assumes, water. *To hell with Ed Abbey. Now it's dry, dry, dry.* Behind her, the trail winds up a hill and straight into the clouds. Before her, the trail descends into the canyon, marked by stacked rocks, promising ruins.

Back to the road, please. Part of her wants to explore. ("That's the difference between you and me—between white people and us," Lance said, driving through the desert one afternoon. "You see that, and you wish you had a tent and a canteen. I grew up with that. It never would have occurred to me to *want* to explore those rocks. I mean, they're rocks. We ran around on them sometimes, sure, but sleep out there?

Why?") More of her wants to turn around, get back on the main highway. Braden is too young to be away from her for very long. Also, no one understands how he eats. He has to mix up textures. Like, tapioca, yes; tofu, no. She's sure Jackie is thinking a lot more about the date she missed than food textures. God knows what sort of havoc Tulip has entertained by now. Yet Gretta can't seem to return to the truck—not yet. She might lose some lesson, some beauty that might carry her through the day. Arrows carry with them a certain insistence; stacked rocks, a weight. *Maybe an ancient somebody will whisper advice in your ear,* she thinks. And, *Yeah, things like, Fuck off, whitey. You're standing on my spot. Go A-Way. Stay A-Way.* Maybe she's just putting off inevitable rejection.

Her conscience hurts for her kids, who, she is sure, have an entirely different message for her. They're old enough now, they'll remember this absence, maybe for the rest of their lives. This week will become a variable in various equations for meaning, possibly for rage. In therapy, it might become central. She raises a toast: *To Mom, Exhibit A.*

Though Tulip commands her mother's attention now, she seemed frighteningly indifferent as a baby. She cried for a couple of seconds when she was born and that was about it. This, despite a cleft palate and lip, which looked so bewildering, so deeply grooved, so fleshy, Gretta assumed it must be painful. Gretta's mother and mother-in-law passed her back and forth. Gretta's mother: "What pretty Oriental eyes. What a sweet button nose. She looks Native American." Lance's mother: "No, no, no. Look at the forehead—and her cheeks! She's just cute. She looks like Gretta. She looks white." They went on like that for a half-hour. "You're my cocoa girl," Lance said to his infant daughter.

Once they took Tulip away for a hearing test, he said to Gretta, "What was that, a sick joke?"

"What?"

"Are you making fun of our daughter? *Tulip?* We agreed we would name her after my mother."

She meant to sneak a different name on the birth certificate, yes, but not to make fun of her daughter. She adored her fetus from the first kick. But once he mentioned it, his point seemed obvious. She hadn't named her Hairlip, but still, Tulip? How could she have missed the implication?

It's my favorite flower...? Instead, she said, "Yeah, well our agreement was six weeks ago—before you disappeared without a trace then showed up conveniently for labor and delivery."

"You kicked me out."

"I didn't think you'd go!"

She didn't kick Lance out when she was pregnant with Braden, and he didn't leave. In fact, she relied heavily on his help, as her hips were so slippery she'd fall every time she got out of bed and her lower back was giving her trouble again. Three weeks after Braden was born they moved into their first house, so Lance was home a lot. He repaired the roof in the middle of winter, painted the walls, installed a new water heater. He grumbled, but he was excited.

Maybe that's what you need—a new old house.

She looks around: no ruins. The sky to the west begins to cloud.

By the time Braden was three months old, Tulip had endured two surgeries and a number of trips to the hospital and clinic for complications and for every cold or flu that passed through town. The scars were so faint, and now, Gretta's mother insisted she looked like Shirley Temple with straight hair, while Lance's mother Renee was proud she looked "almost like a real Indian." She has become her grandmothers' princess and Braden is invisible. The two look alike, but Braden has hazel eyes like her own. Gretta assumes that's why Braden isn't Lance's cocoa boy.

During a fight Lance blamed the hazel eyes on a light-complected Hispanic from their old apartment complex, then took back his words. Tulip and Braden both had Lance's upturned ears. He stayed awake that night, leaning over the crib. "I'm sorry. You're my boy. You're my son."

Lance's family takes their all-Indian heritage very seriously. "But DNA doesn't work like that," Gretta taunted him. "There had to be a white in the basket somewhere. Both sides have to have a recessive gene." She wasn't certain this was true or that she knew, in fact, what a recessive gene could or could not do. She flunked genetics and barely made it through Biology 101 to graduate from college. Also, she had seen a few singers from northern tribes with lighter hair and eyes. Renee was Cheyenne, which was north-ish, wasn't it? *Don't you know anything about history?* But she kept all that to herself, mostly because she was hurt, partly because she was hungry. Lance insisted she was wrong, even when they visited his Aunt Kay on the Wind River Reservation.

Aunt Kay said that one of their ancestors, Blind Warrior, had been married to a woman with red hair. Lance and his sister Sylvia shook their heads no. She said that in addition to Amelia Running Deer Woman, who died of old age, and Runs River, and perhaps a Shakespeare, Black Kettle was married to a white woman from the East. "The people at that time didn't mind marrying more than one woman." Sylvia went into the kitchen, then stood behind her aunt, pulling faces and shaking two empty bottles of Nyquil above her head. James and Darrel laughed; Lance glared at them.

Lance's mother said to her sister, "You have to be careful. This one will write it all down." She nodded toward Gretta.

Aunt Kay didn't seem to hear. She continued, "They say that ghost dance is going to bring a big flood and a wave of mud. All the tribes are going to go way up there to the top of the mountains, and that flood will wash away all the white people. Then things will be the way they used to be. The deer and the rabbits and the buffalo and the birds and the forests, they'll come back, too."

"Don't worry, Gretta. We'll take you with us," Sylvia said, laughing.

"I don't like that story," Lance said. "That guy—Wovoka?—he was raised Mormon, did you know that? It's basically a Mormon story, telling Indians to make nice to the whites."

"Yeah, right. The ghost dance isn't Mormon," Sylvia said. "And what if it was? It's not their fault the government did everything they could to stop it." She turned to Gretta, explained as if out of generosity, "They wanted to stop it because it was so powerful."

"Oh come on, a big flood? A prophet come to save us? Please. Everyone danced and danced, and were we saved?" He gestures to the planks pulled up from Aunt Kay's floors, revealing dirt, to the holes punched into her walls, infested with roaches. Poverty had all but swallowed the woman, so old for her years. "You want to know what your son is doing, hanging out his bedroom window?" he asked his aunt. James motioned for Lance to shut up. "He's selling dope. Prophet come to save us. We need to save ourselves. You want to be a Mormon, Sylvia, go right ahead. I'm no Lamanite. I'm an Indian—what the fuck are you?"

"Watch that language!" Renee snapped. Braden, just seven months old then, began to cry.

"Yeah, you with your white wife and your white house and your white car and your white yard and your white job. You're *so* Indian, aren't you? Go to hell. I never called you a Lamanite."

"Oh, yeah? You go to church. Every Sunday." He sang, "*Book of Mormon stories that my teacher tells to me…are about the Lamanites in ancient history.* I'll bet you sing along, huh?" He laughed the laugh he reserves for true derision—the laugh Gretta had already come to know so personally. "I'll bet you do."

"I go there to see my friends!" Sylvia joined Braden in crying, and Tulip followed suit. "You always have to make trouble, don't you, Lance? Why do you always have to make trouble?"

Since that last trip to Fort Washakie, Gretta has seen genealogy papers a lawyer drew up. Lance's family was in the running for a lawsuit granting reparations to Black Kettle's descendents on account of the indiscriminate slaughter and mutilation of the children, women, and men of his band at Sand Creek and then Custer and the Seventh Cavalry running Black Kettle off a cliff near the Washita River some years later.

That's when Black Kettle did and did not die. When he reached the edge of the cliff, he held his medicine above him, reared his horse, and shouted a war cry before flying off the side of the cliff and disappearing into the trees. According to his story, which was passed down with his belongings, he survived the cavalry's pronouncement of his death; he changed his name and lived in hiding among his people long enough to see Custer go down.

The white woman from the East did not appear on the lawyer's papers, and neither did Blind Warrior.

Later, when Aunt Kay died, Gretta realized she could have patched up the holes in the walls and floors or paid to have it done. She could have cleared the cupboards of the hundreds of neatly stacked NyQuil bottles stored there and replaced them with food. She could have made sure the woman got the insulin she needed in time to save her life, or at least save her right foot so it could have been buried with her. Instead, Gretta took notes. She wrote it all down. She feels it as a reverberation in that damned *front globe* of hers and thinks maybe sin is not just a concept made up to frighten people.

Finally, a small ruin. She realizes suddenly, sadly, that she should have put a bottle of water in her pack. Gin, she suspects, will not do. She should probably not have brought her pack either, because it is making her shoulders ache.

The ruin is almost gone. Gretta is careful to not walk too close, not knowing where the boundaries of the ruin had been.

"You wouldn't walk into someone's house just like that, would you?" Lance's father Clyde had said one night when Gretta talked of camping in the desert, visiting ruins. "All these white people go into their house and take their dish, but you wouldn't see them walking into each other's house. It's the same thing. Those potteries are sacred. That's what they had food on and that's what they used for all kinds of things. You don't understand that kind of sacred. You think the Bible's just the only thing. It's not like that. Those things the Creator gave to us are sacred. The eagle feather. The sage and the sweet grass and the tobacco. And that dish too. Don't touch those things!"

At the moment she feels entirely devoid of creation and any divine delegation of gifts thereof. The Bible—she's never even read it. Agnosticism was inevitable for her, her mother always said, because she wouldn't know what to do with a rule, much less a commandment.

She used to take pride in breaking rules. After being brake-raped by the reckless son of a Qatari diplomat, she said the bit that makes a person become Muslim—for fun, for spite. Nothing happened. Later, she seduced the same man. Twice. The next time she was raped, it was a frat boy. She showed the nurse, two professors, and later a half-filled cafeteria the secret fraternity handshake she made him teach her (after the alcohol but before the incident, of course). Again, nothing happened.

And then there was the business of the mantra. For her sixteenth birthday her aunt introduced her to transcendental meditation. A monkish guy in a blue polyester athletic suit accepted her aunt's offering of thirty-five dollars on Gretta's behalf, then hummed and babbled indiscernibly below a photo of the Maharishi before giving her a mantra. When a scholar from India told her years later that, traditionally, untouchables such as herself weren't supposed to learn any of the systems of yoga, including this pseudo laya yoga ("Maharishi Mahesh Yogi, huh? That's Disneyland. That's Western fools getting their money's worth."), she got drunk and told her brother the secret mantra that had been so ceremoniously whispered into her ear.

And, yes, the ghost. Gretta tried invoking the spirit of Annie Oakley with the Utah Ghost Hunter's Society, specifically against Lance's will. ("It's not our way. You have to be careful what you bring into this house.") She witnessed not a wisp of the supernatural. Actually, the ghost hunters made an ultraslow recording of what they said sounded like, "In your cat lies the fruit." She pointed out that she didn't have a cat. They suggested that maybe it was "In your vat lies the fruit," as in pregnant, but she wasn't pregnant, and having her uterus likened to a vat wasn't her idea of a spiritual encounter.

~ Two Rapids Hotel ~

Fun for the whole famly!

<u>Vat:</u> A large vessel (as a cistern, tub, or barrel) esp. for holding liquors in an immature state or preparations for dyeing or tanning.

<u>Vatic:</u> Seer, prophet; akin to poetry, madness.

<u>Vatu:</u> See MONEY table.

These days, after almost nine years of marriage, it's as if the rules are coming from the inside out.

The canyon bottom, which appears relatively flat beyond the ruin, disappears into a crack about forty yards or so farther south. She walks, then crawls toward the edge. "Now this is a crevice," she says, looking into it. "Crevice. Cravass. Cravass." What's the difference? She can't see the bottom of the V. It makes her ass tickle unbearably. Come November, rain will gush into the crevice. At night it'll freeze, expand. Next year the crevice will be wider. *Or maybe not. Maybe now that the ocean has slipped away, nature is through with this place.*

She wishes she'd kept the roast-beef string so she could measure the crack exactly. Even if she had, she realizes, there's no way to get across. She searches the crevice for evidence of humanity. She drops a pebble in. She hears it glance off one plane and into another, and another, and another, until the sound diminishes to silence. Her teeth ache with the nothingness. She sees as much. No little hands painted on rock. No Coke cans. No squares of discarded toilet paper. *Only the little ruin, and why here, where children can fall through the crevice?*

She gets into her pack to check *Desert Solitaire* for words that might latch on to the surroundings. Reading is the best she can do at the moment. "Suddenly it comes, the flaming globe, blazing on the pinnacles and minarets and balanced rocks, on the canyon walls and through the windows in the sandstone fins. We greet each other, sun and I, across the black void. . . ."

It sounds like poetry. *Sentimentally yours.* This alliance with the sun, this disregard for the void—it annoys her. It's not that she doesn't like Ed Abbey or the rugged individual for which he stands. The thing that angers her is that she shares an appreciation for the desert yet can't seem to write such love letters—not even to a landscape. She both resists the sentimentality and wishes she could be a part of it. He speaks so adoringly, so openly...what if she were to embrace—*Do you have to use that word?*—anything, anyone so pointedly? Pinnacles, minarets, fins—what's the difference? By what quality is each defined? *By observation.* By love.

But what will the rock formations be, once the land is overtaken by oil drills, by overpopulation? Rubble? Props in a mall? *Wife, lover, significant other, significant mother.* To what end? So maybe it's true: Great-great Grandpa whisked away Great-great Grandma, saving her from the brutality of shit-assed johns and lavishing her with words of love. The man died in a gutter on 25th Street in Ogden, Utah, and the woman sought sanctuary with friends and only a decade later died of tuberculosis in a brothel on the same street, according to her grandma.

Rocks. Even if she found a shard of pottery, she supposes she wouldn't touch it. There is something that excites her about finding a piece of pottery, though—it looks like any old piece of clay on the one side and art on the outside. You pick the piece up, as if with naiveté, and turn it over. The black lines on gray or white almost stand in place of magic, as if the fingers that put them there were, more than fingers, god-fingers. You tuck the piece under a sticker bush, knowing that in a few years the area will be so raked over by adventurists, there will be none left. The pieces will be disseminated into many a drawer of useful and forgotten things only to break in half, then into several pieces, then into a scattering of crumbs. *Semantically ours.*

She doesn't have such artifacts. She does have three handmade bowls from Japan. The fourth is still at her grandmother's house. Her grandpa brought them back from World War II. "With all those pictures of little Jap children," her grandma said. "They looked like the cutest damned monkeys. Even with some of them their arms chopped off or with one leg." Lance makes excuses for her, but Gretta knows the truth—her grandmother is still angry about Pearl Harbor. Or more accurately, about the Japanese lover her grandfather took during the war.

~ Two Rapids Hotel ~

Fun for the whole famly!

Clouds accumulate in the west, making a slight, if ubiquitous, rumbling.

There, she thinks. *That's my poetry. That's my love.* But it doesn't mean anything. There could be a cloudburst here and nowhere else. More likely, the clouds will dissipate before the hour, because that's the way the desert is.

She rolls onto her back, staring up at the west wall of the canyon. At first it is more of the same, then it takes shape—seven, eight, nine kivas. At least. A village, tucked coyly into the cliffside, wooden posts sticking out of the red walls of stacked rock. Her heart races and her eyes water. If eleven people fit in a little trailer house, how many could live in a kiva? She looks for a trail leading up to the structures, but eventually, she gives in and feels only relief. Even her yearning for the old Leica wanes. *I will never,* she thinks, smiling mentally if not measurably, *touch that dish.* The cliffside is beautiful as it is—golden, imperfect, transparent, and long untouched.

Second Place Is Pretty Good, Considering

THE SIGHT of the truck is as comforting as it is disconcerting. Gretta rips the paper plate off the fence, wads it up, and throws it through the window into the backseat. She pees at the side of the truck, curses the drip-dry method of dripping wet until less wet. She should have prepared herself with a wipe before urinating. In the console, she finds both the wipes and two pints of Gilbey's. She wipes belatedly with a baby wipe, considers the fact that now would be a good time to quit drinking gin and drink lots of water. For that matter, there must be something to wipe with that Al Gore would feel more comfortable with—biodegradable toilet paper? In other countries, a hand. If you wipe with your hand then sanitize your hand, does that mean you've added to the planet not a wipe but some strange sanitizing chemical? An ignorance that leaves her with the one option: dripping wet until less wet. She pours herself a little cocktail with more tonic than gin, a compromise, and boots up.

DearJames.doc

p.p.s. ~~It's not that I didn't like your gesture. I mean, he's your brother. How was I supposed to react?~~

I didn't send a dictionary so you would check your spelling. I sent it to you because I thought you might like it.

p.p.p.s. A few weeks ago I took the kids to the Utah State powwow. Tulip placed second in her new jingle dress. Please write to congratulate her. If you talk to anyone in your family, send them the same message. It would mean a lot to her—sometimes she feels forgotten.

M.Butterfly.doc

L. leads her into the arena.

G: I had a vision. Of matrimony. That, deep within his almond eyes, there was acceptance. He would see me not as a lack of pigment but for who I was: his wife. A wife, even, who had carried his children.

L. takes her hand and dances with her, an owl dance.

G: Dancing with his wife would be better than having an affair with a Navajo lover, wouldn't it? (*G. stops dancing, shakes her head.*) The love of a spouse can withstand many things—unfaithfulness, that crevice. Even abandonment. But how can it face the one sin that implies all others? The devastating knowledge that, underneath it all, his wife is nothing more, nothing less than…a white girl.

A Little Reluctance Goes a Long Way

GRETTA IS smoking a cigarette and browsing the dictionary on the tailgate when an old white Corolla pulls over. It is the second car she has seen since a sprinkling of rain cleared up, leaving its scent. She gets up to see who it is. The passenger door of the car opens. A man gets out. The trunk is popped open and the man gets a duffel bag out of it. The man leans back into the car for a moment then shuts the door. The Corolla drives off. "Fuck you too, motherfucker!" the man shouts after the car. The voice is familiar. The man begins walking toward her.

Gretta is pretty sure she feels nervous, but double-checks—shortness of breath, fuzzy forehead. If she were in the movies, she might back up. She might hop out of the bed of the truck and get in the cab, she might— *If you were in the movies, you wouldn't leave, because that's where the story would end.* Curious/attracted—which? This sort of confusion has been a problem for some years now—afraid/excited, dedicated/addicted, disillusioned/exhausted. In this case, she opts for curious. Her mother would not approve; neither would Lance.

"Hey!" he yells. It is him—the tequila man.

Her lifeforce vanishes and returns as quickly, with a raging fever. *Don't be afraid.*

"Figment," she reads aloud. "Something made up or contrived."

"Did you plan this?" he says, approaching the truck slowly. "I thought that was you—this pickup is hard to miss." He pats the yellow door and grins. She weighs the probabilities. *A sound beating? A good ass-chewing?*

"Would you like a gin-and-tonic?" Despite her fear, she feels good she is such a nice hostess, given the circumstances—that he jabbed at her pathos, that she ditched him on the highway, that she saw him naked, *that he—*

"A little early, isn't it?" he asks. He doesn't appear vengeful. Actually, he seems more calm than when she met him. A little more handsome, maybe. Taller.

"It's got to be going on five o'clock. Have a better idea?"

"Not really, no. I could use a drink." He looks around, watches ravens fly overhead. "Shouldn't you be in Arizona by now?"

Might this constitute The Romance? she wonders. *This return to the cad?*

He returned to you, Gretta. She checks her breasts—no swelling. No creaming, no firming. She attempts an assessment of her emotions—she's pretty sure she's not feeling the love that would toss her back into the dreaded genre, but how would she know? All emotions feel the same to her—intensity, anxiety, a gnarling of the innards. She smiles, despite her concern.

"I've been waylaid."

"Yeah? By what?" he says.

She gestures toward him as if he is a *Price Is Right* prize.

"That's not getting laid. I can *show* you getting laid."

Herpes, hepatitis, AIDS. "Thanks, but no. I've been thinking about what you said. That maybe I should move on. Or…I don't know. I'm thinking. I'm thinking I'm moving on. Like, no more fucking up. Also, car trouble."

"Truck trouble," he says. He takes a 360° at the flat, washed-out desert around him. "Where are we?"

"South of Monticello, I think. Between Monticello and Cortez. I ought to know the place like the back of my hand. I seem to be pinballing back and forth between the two."

She takes the bottles of gin and tonic out of the cab and arranges them with the hotel's plastic cups on the tailgate. "I don't have a lime. I know how you like a lime." She rummages through the glove compartment. "I have this," she says, shaking a green plastic lime-shaped bottle of lime juice. "I don't have a straw or ice."

"Enough," he says. "You owe me a big fucking apology. My feet are killing me. Not to mention—"

"I forgot to catch your name," she says.

"Two pints? Why don't you just buy a fifth?"

"Easier to hide."

He fixes both of them a drink, then sits on the ground, leaning back on his hands, his ankles crossed. "You're lucky someone picked me up not long after you dumped me off. Otherwise I'd have to cut you up into tiny pieces and throw you in the river."

Gretta is pretty sure he's joking, but his statement does call into question the wisdom of picking up hitchhikers—and then getting oral sex from them—in the first place. She thinks about asking him where he's from and how he got here. She decides she doesn't want to know where's he's from or where he's going. If anything, she wants to know whether he liked their foreplay, or whether he has sores in his mouth. She wants to know if he uses hair gel to get his curly fuzzy mane like that. If she managed to fantasize about loveless consensuality as she had protected sex, would she still be securely in violation of The Romance? *So long as the breasts don't swell, yeah?*

"Starter's dead," she tells him.

"Good for you," he says.

"If you can fix it, I'll give you a ride—anywhere on my bee line."

"Fix it?" He laughs. "Fix a starter? Out here? With what, a magic wand?"

"Come on, you're a guy."

He gets up, brushes gravel off the seat of his pants, and stretches. He leans over her and kisses her, motivated and focused and tasting of toothpaste. She flies off a cliff and disappears into the trees. "I'm not a guy—I'm a *man*." He returns to his drink, shining clear and bright on the pavement. She touches her lip where his tooth nicked it. She feels thick and small and sick to her stomach. *And what would that be?*

Threatened? Hungover? Shocked. She is shocked by the difference in his kiss. She doesn't remember what it's like to be kissed by someone besides Lance.

"There's no fixing a starter in the middle of nowhere, sweetheart," he says. "What'd you do to it?"

"I didn't *do* anything. It's been having trouble turning over for a while—a week, maybe two. You heard it. Last time I went to start it, I kept hearing a noise, kind of a click, like. Anyway, I tried again and it was fine. But this time...nothing."

"Bad karma."

"Got any more of that toothpaste?" she asks.

"You look like you slept in a morgue," he says.

"I think I did." Possibilities enter her feet and crawl up her thighs like runs in nylons. She wonders whether he might fall for the same trick twice. She has heard of a thing called a female condom; whatever it is, it won't help her now—not unless he has one, and if he carries one, he would have used it before. *Wouldn't he have?*

"Show me happy and I'll give you some toothpaste. You could use it."

"Excuse me," she says, ambling to the front of the truck, where she thinks she might vomit. Nothing comes. She squats in front of the grill and drools a little. He walks up behind her and asks if she's okay. He strokes her hair back away from her face until it's apparent she's not going to throw up.

"Here," he says, giving Gretta the bottle of tonic.

"Thanks. I don't feel so good."

"If it weren't me you dropped off naked, I would say that was pretty funny, what you did."

"You're not mad?"

"Of course I'm mad. No wonder your husband left you—you can be a real bitch."

She tries to get up and smile, but it doesn't work like she thought it would. He sits next to her and talks about things like the death of vinyl records and how to put a stop to spam and viruses. She pretends that she doesn't know much about the Internet just so she can hear him talk.

"…And never, never go to a porn site or an Rx site. You'll have no end to pop-ups. My wife was ready to kill me."

"You're married?"

"Was. Don't sound so shocked."

Cars pass. They wave, with the effect of a parade wave. He pulls a miniature tube of Crest out of his pocket and gives it to her. "It's yours," he says. "You can use my toothbrush."

Teeth clean, she explains: "I'm not entirely pathetic, you know. Not really." She talks about her job as if it were a good job. She mentions a scholarship, honors. More cars pass. No one stops.

"How's your cut?" she says after a long silence.

"Same." He shows her. The blood has been cleaned off the wound, which, Gretta sees, is not much more than a deep scratch, but the bruise on his chest looks awful.

"You should put some gin on it. Or maybe tonic water is good for that kind of thing." He shakes his head no. "You tired?" she says.

"I'm not up for walking yet, if that's what you mean. Let's take a nap. We take a nap, then we clean you up. People are more likely to pick up a girl. You're just the ticket."

"Girl?"

"Oh, get over yourself, will you?"

"How about guy. Oh, I'm sorry—*man*."

"Woman, then."

"It'll be dark before long. They won't pick us up in the dark."

"Just a little nap?"

She gets the quilt out of the cab. "On it or under it?"

"On it. No, under it."

"Hey, I need a favor," she says.

"Get naked? Oh, I know! Get you a towel."

"I need you to talk to someone for me. Her name is Jackie. Tell her I'm all right. You're a driver for a towing company—are you listening?—and you helped me get to a mechanic."

"Who's this we're calling? Jackie?"

"You towed my pickup because it was broken down and I left my cell phone in your truck."

"Why don't you call her?"

"It's complicated. Let's see…I left the phone in your truck…how would you know to call?"

"You called on the toll-free number on my business card and asked me to call."

"I was stranded all night and all day, and I didn't call earlier because my cell phone was out of range…and then I didn't call when you picked me up because…"

"Too much detail," he says.

"All right. Just…just play it by ear."

She dials for him. "Yes, this is an axe-murderer. I'm calling about Gretta…." He grins. "Just kidding. No answer—ah, wait, answering machine." He clears his throat and assumes a southern accent. "Yeah, hi. This is Bobby Billthorpe from Bobby Billthorpe Towing. I just picked up a friend of your'n by the name of Gretta…" He looks at her for help. She mouths *Bitsilly.* "…Gretta Bit Silly. She wants you to know she's safe and happy as a clown. She left her cell phone—" He stops, raises his eyebrows. "I ran out of time," he says to her. "Do you want me to call again and leave another message?"

"No, that was good."

"What if they try to call?"

"Just turn it off. I'll call tomorrow."

They climb in the bed of the pickup. He lays down a fleece jacket and suggests Gretta use it as a cushion. He rests his head on her pack, closes his eyes. *No creaming. No firming.* She rests her head on his stomach and watches him breathe until sleepiness begins to take over. *No tomorrow, no yesterday.* He pets strands of hair behind her ear with big clumsy fingers until it's all tucked neatly away, and then they sleep.

I Want Some Cookies

"HEY!"

Gretta wakes up with the sun in one ear and a rumbling in the other. Despite the protestations of his stomach, the tequila man is still asleep.

"You!"

Gretta sits up. "Hey," she says to the elderly couple standing beside the truck. She stands up in the bed and scratches her arms.

"You kids okay?"

It takes Gretta a minute to think about what the man is asking. She sees parked ahead of her a Wilderness trailer plastered with WE'RE SPENDING OUR CHILDREN'S INHERITANCE bumper stickers.

The tequila man stretches. "Good morning," he says.

"Got troubles?" asks the old man. "Your emergency lights are on."

"I think my starter is broken," she says.

"You sure it ain't your battery?" he asks.

"I don't think so. I mean, the radio works and all that. And, I guess, the emergency lights."

"Got any cookies on you?"

"Carl!" the woman says.

"Damned right. I want some cookies."

"We don't have any cookies," says the tequila man. Gretta notices his hair is even fuzzier than it was before. She tries not to laugh.

"Well, hell. I'll see you two later."

"Carl!"

"I'm just pulling their leg, honey. Come on, young man. Let's see what we can do."

The tequila man disappears up the road and inside the trailer and emerges with a Diet Pepsi and a long piece of black licorice. He follows the old man back to the truck. "Now just you watch. Maybe you'll learn something."

He lies down beside the truck. "When I tap, you turn the ignition. You listening? All right then." He climbs under and taps. The ignition resists. "Let's try her again!" He taps some more. Reluctantly, the ignition turns over. He scoots out and the tequila man steps onto the pavement. "You're going to have to get that starter replaced pronto," he says.

His wife adds, "This trick'll work once, twice, maybe a dozen times, but pretty soon, that'll be all she wrote. You can also jimmy a screwdriver…well, just get to a mechanic. Life will get a whole lot easier."

"That's my Julie. First-rate mechanic," the man says proudly.

They all shake hands. The old man professes that he, too, is a Chevy man. The tequila man asks for a ride.

"You're going to split up—just like that?" the woman asks, her hand shading her eyes from the morning sun.

"It's his decision," Gretta says. She feels like she should apologize.

"So…you're not together?" says the old man, wagging his finger back and forth between them. The tequila man shrugs. "Well, hell, I thought you were married. Where you going?" the old man asks.

He shrugs again. "South?"

"All right. Long as you ride in the trailer. Don't think I won't put you to work. Ever see Bryce Canyon? A playground for angels and demons." He winks at Gretta and ushers the tequila man away.

"Wait!" Gretta runs to the cab for the rest of her pack of Oreos. She runs back to the old man.

"Well, aren't you a sweetheart?" he says. "Hey, I like the broken ones." He takes the cookies and pats her arm. "Straight to a mechanic, now."

The tequila man smiles, waves, fades, and disappears. Gretta suddenly remembers that at least one emotion makes itself perfectly clear.

Who's Your Butterfly?

M.Butterfly.doc

L. takes her hand and dances with her, an owl dance.

G: Dancing with his bloated sunburned pasty-assed smoke-smelling wife would be better than ~~having an affair with a~~ fucking a likely young, likely attractive Navajo lover, wouldn't it? *(G. stops dancing, shakes her head.)* The ~~love~~ affections of a spouse can withstand many things—unfaithfulness, ~~that crevice~~ loss. Even ~~abandonment~~ neediness. But how can it face the one sin that implies all others? The devastating knowledge that, underneath it all, his wife was nothing more, nothing less than...a drunk ~~white girl~~.

The truck is getting hot and smells of smashed fox foot. Gretta is too sauced to care about that. She feels free in such close vicinity to ruin. She wants desperately to call her kids, hear their voices. "Night-night, Mom," Braden might say. Or, "Who dis?" And Tulip: "I hate you and I always will." *Oh, come on, has she ever said that?*

The only time she feels brave enough to call, she has had enough to drink that Tulip would pick it up in an instant and tell her she'll tell her dad—or at least Jackie. Instead, Gretta opts for the void. She considers staying in this state of being, then remembers Braden has to be enrolled in the Li'l Tigers by next week. *Maybe I'm not so close to ruin,* she thinks. *Maybe I'm a boring mom with a boring life and a husband who doesn't love her. I ought to buy slippers.*

KeepOut.doc

Lance's parents for the weekend. Tulip was still a baby. We walked in the door, family room was filled with about a dozen white people and as many Indians (I recognized a couple), a few Hispanics, and a black couple. Southeast Idaho had never seen such diversity. Thought it was somebody's birthday or a retirement party. Card tables were set up with pretzels and fry bread and Jell-O fruit salad and two-liters of pop.

"Gretta! Let me introduce you to our friends." Some were neighbors, some outpatients from Second Chance (Clyde was their sponsor), some from Fort Hall. The black couple was originally from Kenya, more recently Idaho Falls. When Lance shook everyone's hand, I did too, and all I could think about was germs. I felt bad, but I didn't want to take Tulip back to the hospital again. Seemed like she picked up something every time we went anywhere—school, store, library, friends' houses. The last person was a white woman—she patted my hand, said, "Renee has told us so much about you."

Clyde: "We were just about to play cards." Renee: "You never came to our house on a Thursday, have you?"

I asked Lance what was going on.

"They do this every Thursday," he said.

"Since when?"

"Since always."

"Why didn't you tell me?"

"Tell you what?"

Tell me what. That his parents weren't necessarily separatists. That obviously something was wrong with Gretta besides her race. If it wasn't color, what was it? She always thought it was bad news they hated her for being white. Worse news to know she had to keep digging. And what was Renee saying about her to others? If it were something good, something sincere, Gretta would have to rethink everything. If it were something bad…surely it was something bad.

```
Went to bathroom to breastfeed. Tulip wasn't hun-
gry, but I couldn't move. Renee knocked after about
a half hour, yelling, "It's not too late to buy in.
Three dollars buys your chips."
```

If she'd been wrong about Lance's parents being separatists, what else had she got wrong? *What have I got wrong now?*

This is Gretta's life at home: She gets up at six and feels like it's the first time she has ever gotten up at six, and she straightens the house. That is, she makes the house arguably less messy. She washes her face, brushes her teeth. She wakes up the kids and dresses them. Lance used to feed the kids in the morning, but now Gretta puts the cereal in reach so Tulip can take care of that. If they don't want to eat, she doesn't make them. She ignores the crying and the moaning. She doesn't have the energy to do otherwise. By seven-thirty, she should be out the door, though she never is. She throws on clothes and shoes and stuffs whatever she is unable to assemble on the kids into a bag, along with snack-pack peaches or pears. She pushes everything and everyone into the truck, drives to daycare, still ignoring the cries and the moans. At some point, the nasty Folgers kicks in and her eyes get buggy. She ignores the day-care workers, who remind her she has to pay up or quit bringing Braden. She doesn't say a word—not anymore. She kisses Braden good-bye as he clings to her leg and cries. She peels him off her leg, runs to the car like a bank robber, and reminds herself she doesn't have the luxury of quitting her job. She takes Tulip down the street to Lakeview Elementary. She asks her daughter for her goal for the day—for the tidbit of information she's always wanted to know that she can look up during library time. Once she has prodded something out of her, she kisses her good-bye.

She goes to work and pretends that she is not a sellout. She pretends that her boss is not an arrogant bastard with such a sense of entitlement, the mountains pull back when he walks out the door. She cranks out text as if she were not the one who wrote it. Time goes by without her. She is on hold. People go to lunch without her; she eats her peaches, her pears. The indoor-outdoor carpet beneath her feet (speckled blue, as if the fluorescent lights aren't torturous enough) thins her out in an irrevocable sort of way. She turns on the heat to counteract the air conditioning. Her coworkers come back, complain that it's hot, and turn the air conditioning back on.

She is ever on hold. Type, type, type.

Eventually, it is four forty-five. She pays an embittered parking-lot attendant and drives to day care. She ignores the workers as they ask her if she's going to pay next time and give her a talk on the meaning of good faith. She pretends that Braden is not crying because he hates day care. She picks up Tulip from the after-school program. She drives them all home, stops for anything that costs about a dollar per person—on-special hamburgers, tacos, corn dogs, whatever. On good days they eat inside, in the play area. On bad days, she gets it to go and begs the kids to shut up and get in the car, where they eat in silence. Then they go home, go over Tulip's homework, and wait. What they are waiting for, she doesn't know. For Lance, she supposes. But night after night, Lance does not show up. The TV and books fail to inspire her, with rare exception. She hasn't had the money or babysitting to go to the darkroom for months. She sometimes gets the kids started on projects—toothpick forts, milk-jug birdfeeders—but always ends up yelling about something, making the kids feel uncomfortable and worse off than had they just watched cartoons. Friends do not call, because no friend will endure her inability to return calls, to learn her lesson. Well, she has Jackie—or had, depending on how angry she is about the babysitting. But Jackie is busy being single and childless; Gretta can't accompany her on raft trips or to Reiki workshops, gallery strolls, pub crawls. She wouldn't have the energy, even if she were granted time, money, and a babysitter by a fairy godmother.

She has the dictionary. Of course, there's no forcing the dictionary to render tolerable—much less excitable—words on the most dreary of days.

Often she has medicine to concentrate on, because the kids are always sick from something they picked up at school or daycare. She arranges and rearranges bottles of generic Benadryl, Triaminic,

Robitussin. She doles out vitamins like they're candy, because she knows the nutrition her kids get is only slightly better than the nutrition she gets, and her hair is frazzled, her nails thin as paper. Later she finds Tulip's vitamins hidden between couch cushions.

That is my life, she thinks. *That is my motherhood.* She feels a terrible loss, and she can't say exactly what for. Maybe for the integrity that preceded self-pity. *Or did it ever?* She blames it all on Lance. For the moment, she can at least do that.

WordsforLater.doc

Lance: A steel-tipped spear carried by mounted knights or light cavalry. Any of various sharp objects suggestive of a lance. To pierce with or as if with a lance. To throw forward: HURL. To move forward quickly.

In Drills and Bursts

"YOU HAVING another one of them damned things?"

"No. I just called to say hi. Just…I miss you."

"You never did tell me the end of that story. Don't hang up on me again, you little shit. I can't stand it—it makes me worry. Your mother and dad are worried to death as it is, so I didn't even mention you called."

"What story?"

"Last time you called me. Let's see—a woman drives up to an evangelist's house and demands proof of something or other, and instead they give her a jar of apricots and a brochure, tell her she'd damned well better repent because the last days are coming."

"I don't know what you're talking about, Grandma."

"Oh, kiddo."

"I'm sorry."

"No need to be sorry. They always say that, and the last days *are* coming—for all of us. We're all born, we all die.… You still heading to see those colorful people?"

"People of color, Grandma. You can call them American Indian or Native American."

She once called Lance an Injun and he gave her a gentle talk on political correctness. He has an affection for the woman that has been, at some moments, greater than her own. He lets her tell stories for hours—even when they're about her mother hiding under her great-aunt's skirts "when the natives came a-calling."

"What's taking you so long, Gretchen? What is it?"

"I don't know. I got almost there, real close, and I had to drive back to find a mechanic. That's all I seem to be able to do. Drive back and forth, back and forth. I just can't seem to get there."

"Button, Button."

"Who's got the mutton."

"You think you can call my house and tell Jackie I'm all right, I'm just getting the truck fixed? Tell her I'm sorry I haven't called her myself. I'm having a hard time."

"I don't think the kids are staying at your house."

"What do you mean? Where are they?"

"Calm down. The kids are with your mother. Jackie went home."

"Why?"

"You're going to have to take that up with her."

"All right. Okay. So how have you been?"

Gretta snivels into the cell phone while her grandma talks about the visiting teachers from her ward. "I know they don't like my smoke, but you know, they never have said a word."

"Why would they? They're lesbians."

"They're not lesbians."

"You don't think?"

"No. And if they was, what would that have to do with smoking?"

"They'd know how to keep to themselves about things that are forbidden, I guess."

"No one forbids me to do anything. I'm sure they'll line up to do my temple work after I croak, but until then, I live my life like a big girl. You remember that. Live the life you want to live because you have no idea what comes after."

Gretta wishes she knew what kind of life she wanted—maybe she would live it. "I have to go now." Her voice, she is sure, reveals her as the blubbering fuckup that she is. *You're pathetic.* She had to backtrack north once more—back to find a mechanic. One of Monticello's two mechanics was on vacation and the other was closed on weekends. Cortez shops were either booked up or closed for the weekend. One guy was available but wanted two hundred dollars for a remanufactured starter, plus labor at seventy-five dollars an hour; he took nearly a half-hour to go to the restroom, check his inventory for the starter, and calculate an indefinite estimate. She called mechanics in Shiprock and got no answer. So Moab, it was. Moab again. She is certain this is the longest trip south anyone has ever taken. Eighteenth-century explorers must have made better time.

"The truck should be ready soon."

"You can always come home. We'll have a few beers, play Penny-Annie like we used to. You remember that? 'Just one more game, Grandma.' It was always just one more game. Don't worry about your mom—I'll take care of her. She's just worried about you, that's all. We all are. You and the kids can settle down in the basement.... Sell the house—it's a monkey on your back.... Gretta, honey, you can always come home."

Gretta stares at her phone for a while after she disconnects—two messages. She hadn't noticed. And now that she has—*Forget it.* She sits listening to the drills and bursts of air—to whatever metallic sprites make up the nerve-stripping racket of an auto shop—and tries to compose herself. A woman in a tittie tank and camouflage shorts sits across from her. Gretta imagines running her hand up the woman's small defined calves to see how closely she shaves. The woman, however, picks out of a stack of last year's magazines an issue of *Time* with a favorable-looking image of President Bush on the cover. Gretta scowls. The woman, catching her gaze, scowls back.

Gretta opens the laptop with good intentions, but she has nothing to say. Instead she reads something she has already written.

October1997.doc

We drove up a dirt road through a field. We pulled up to a log cabin the size of my mother's walk-in closet. "You lived there?" I asked. "For seven years," Renee said. "Me and my sisters and brothers and my mother and father. Halfway up that hill, my youngest brother died. And right over there, my other brother. And down over there, my dad. My mom would walk around the house at night crying. There's a way women cry when they've lost something. We tried not to listen. Then me and two of my sisters were sent to the Catholic school. My brothers and other sisters that were left stayed home and died from the sickness."

We were on the Wind River Reservation in Wyoming. There were fields and fields of dead grass or maybe it's something people eat, I couldn't tell the difference. The blanket that was the door hung to the side from a nail. On one side of the cabin, there was a sky-blue wall. There was a window with no glass. In the middle of the cabin, taking up most of the space, a metal twin-sized bed. A yellowed striped mattress, which had been gutted through a hole near the middle, lay halfway on the wire coils, halfway off the bed. A wood stove with no stovepipe, in the front corner of the cabin, sat dangerously close to the bed. A handmade cupboard stood against the west wall, one cupboard door open. On the shelves were an empty can of oil, pages of a magazine, cobwebs, dead bees and flies, and a paper cup. Renee added a can opener, six cans of corn, six cans of green beans, a case of chili beans, a bottle of aspirin, and a case of bottled water.

On the walls were penned and penciled journals, slanting up, slanting down.

"Who did this?" I asked.

"My brother still stays here sometimes—when he's around. I left him some blankets last time. I don't know where they are," she said.

1962 Mom died. Cold. Hungry.

1968 didn't drink today, lonely—

1976 went to Idaho

1978 took a drink today. Hungry.

Decbr. Been sober six days. I'm lonely. Pow Wow at hi-school

It was okay.

Cold. Hungry. Went to Idaho to harvest. Irving dyed.

> The notes were everywhere. I couldn't read them all. I took a few pictures, but I felt strange—was this place sacred like the sweat lodge, off-limits to cameras? A cultural anthropologist would be crazy not to preserve and study it. I pulled my fingertips off the words—was it like the pottery, not to be touched? My husband and sister-in-law walked around the outside of the cabin. My mother-in-law and her sister Kay leaned against the doorframe, made of two-by-fours. No one said anything about my camera, so I shot.
>
> *1982 Aug Visited Aunt S. She looked real big.*
>
> *1994 It got cold today.*
>
> *Septembr '66 hungry. Going to harvest with Benny.*
>
> *1996 Sober 6 mo. Til today. Liz finish high school. Mom went to hospital—kidnees.*
>
> Twelve children were raised in this space. Then it came, the sickness. Like an iron fist, or a slow leak.

And there it is again—remorse, futility. Gretta could have replaced the mattress, at least with one from a yard sale or thrift store. She could have brought in another blanket—could have made her home available, for that matter. Instead, she shot pictures, which brings to mind Lance's problem with scientists: privileging anthropology or archeology over people and place.

She shuts down the laptop and stares at the little screen of her phone, at the two blinking envelopes. It can't be good—she can't think of a message she'd want. *But maybe it's Tulip. Could be Lance.*

"Call me. Bill." And the next: *click.* She checks caller ID. William Malberry and Unavailable.

"Shit," she says to the woman reading *Time.* "It's Bill." She returns his call. By the fourth ring, she is ready to hang up ("*I tried to reach you...*"), but hears his voice.

"Hey, Bill."

"Hey, Gretta. Hey, I don't know how to say this."

The woman watches her from above her magazine. She smiles to dam up any potential tears, because she knows what's coming. It's as if she always has.

"Yes, you do."

"The team and I have been talking, discussing matters, so to speak. You're not being fired. Your job, however, is being eliminated. Cutbacks. Economy. But…I talked to your mother…."

"You what?"

"We're not cutting you off. No, we're—we're trying this from a freelance point-of-view. For now. That is, if you're willing to give it your all. This could benefit you, Gretta. It could be the best thing that ever happened to you, what with your quirky schedule and being a single mom and all."

"Fuck."

"I know you need the money. And I know Lance isn't dead. Let it go, Gretta. Just let it go. I'll pay you double what our regular freelancers get until you get back on your feet. Let's say, eight or nine weeks? Then we can reassess the rate and come up with a solution that works for all of us."

"Double your usual rate? Oh, so twelve cents a word? Shit." She has heard CHIPS enrollment has already closed. Without insurance, she'll have to take the kids to the reservation doctor in Fort Hall two and a half hours away.

"Who knows, it might inspire you to set your goals a little higher, meet your deadlines…. Gretta? Hello?"

"I have a week of sick leave—"

"Of course. We'll get you paid for anything you're owed. Don't you worry. And Gretta? There's a good counselor in my ward if you need one. I don't think I've ever told you, but my sister had a little problem with substance abuse."

"Jesus!"

Time sighs, puts her magazine down, and picks Gretta's phone up from the floor. She hands it to her as delicately as if it were a baby bird. "Maybe it's best," she says. "These cancer phones bring out the worst in people."

Rubber Hatchets

AFTER GRETTA maxes out a credit card on the starter, she has, by her estimation, three good cards left. She spends the remainder of one on a big clay salad bowl for her mother, on a white-shell necklace for her grandma and a turquoise bracelet for Jackie, and for the kids she buys T-shirts, rubber animals, turquoise-and-onyx rings, a Bugs Bunny lunch box for Tulip, an Incredible Hulk lunch box for Braden. She fills the lunch boxes with retro candy—Boston Baked Beans, Astro Pops, Charleston Chews, Lemonheads. In a wave of mean-spiritedness that she hopes is directed toward Lance, she throws in plastic bows and arrows, rubber hatchets, and Minnetonka moccasins. For herself, she buys a small bottle of oil that smells of azaleas.

"Got any batons?" she asks the cashier. To her surprise, she does. One with glittery tassels on the ends. It's not much, it's not professional, but it must be better than a chair leg. She buys two so the kids won't fight over the one.

"I'll need your card again."

Gretta used to bead the kids' moccasins and make all of their dance outfits. Once Lance left, she stopped. She tried taking the kids to a powwow by herself, but she felt out of place and so did the kids. Almost a month ago, Renee sent Tulip a new jingle dress, which came to them as a complete shock after so many months of no contact, so Gretta took her and Braden to a small powwow at the Indian Walk-in Center. As they drove through the parking lot, Tulip admitted, "It doesn't feel right without Dad. Do we have to go in?"

They did go in. Tulip danced. She won by default, with only two jingle-dress dancers in her age category, even though she missed intertribal dances and grand entry, and on the last song she practically gave up and stood there, barely dancing with her feet. She cried, embarrassed, and asked for her dad.

Gretta tried to send their outgrown dance outfits to the Salvation Army, but she couldn't do it. It seemed they should be kept in the family. With no real hope for another baby and no contact with her in-laws, though, there were no children to pass them to. Instead, she kept them in a box with a cedar block. They seemed buried alive, so she put them in the attic. Still they haunted her.

"Um…this time the machine is saying declined," says the cashier.

"Here, this one's good," she says, handing over another card. "You know where the post office is?"

She makes it to the post office just before it closes. She sends the packages overnight express—if she doesn't make it home right away, she'll need to please people who would otherwise be angry with her.

I'm Saying If

GRETTA PULLS into Golden Granary between two jeeps covered in sandy red mud. *Just hang up.* A driver sits in the jeep to her left. He looks at her, winks. She waves a pinky finger from her cell phone, thinking the man must be desperate. *Just hang up, Gretta.*

"I'm not sure what you're asking, ma'am."

"I'm saying *if* I accidentally drank more alcohol than I thought I drank, what would happen if I took my Dilantin? I mean, I think I have an idea, but I want to be sure."

"Are you saying you drank alcoholic beverages while taking Dilantin?"

"I'm saying if." She can't go into the store like this. She needs a brush, a rubber band, a hat—something. She needs a tooth-brushing. *You need to go in that store if you want to buy any of those things.* She should have called a different pharmacy than the one she plans to go into.

"Drinking alcoholic beverages is not recommended while taking phenytoin."

"That's why I'm calling, see. I'm saying what will happen if—"

"We recommend that you limit or cease alcohol intake while taking phenytoin."

"Yes, I know. But I'm talking yesterday. I drank. I mean, there was a wedding, they had this tropical punch, I knew it tasted funny, but it was a Hawaiian-themed wedding, what with the fruit. . . ."

Or perhaps she should have paid for the prescription, then asked. *Stupid. Stupid.*

"Let me see if I understand what you're asking. You drank alcohol while taking phenytoin—"

"If. . . ."

"You've taken the Dilantin and—"

"I mean I haven't taken the Dilantin! I drank the alcohol."

"If you miss a dose—"

"Five. I missed five doses. Seven maybe. Extended release."

Another young man joins the first in the jeep. They talk. They look over, wave. The driver revs the engine, and they're off. Friendly place, Moab.

"Five doses or more?"

"Right, since Friday."

"You can't just go off phenytoin like that. You have to go off it gradually."

"I'm saying, can I. . .*may* I please speak to the pharmacist?"

"This is the pharmacist and I'm saying you can't—we don't *recommend* that you discontinue use suddenly. You should probably see your physician immediately."

"Look, I have one. Simple. Question. What happens if I drink—a lot—*and* take my Dilantin? The doctor told me I shouldn't, so I haven't. . .drank a whole lot. . .usually. . .until recently. . . ."

"Let's see. . . . 'Acute alcoholic intake may increase phenytoin serum levels while chronic alcohol use may decrease—"

"I mean! I'm sorry to yell. I'm not yelling. I've read the insert. I know the short answer. Now I want the real answer. Will I twitch around? Will I breathe okay?"

"The alcohol will alter the medication's effectiveness—"

"But in not taking it, I'm definitely altering the medication's effectiveness. So am I better off taking some than none, or what? Should I double up?"

"How much alcohol—what did you say your name was?"

Gretta snaps her phone shut, bangs it against the steering wheel, waits for an ebb. An ebb doesn't present itself.

What is it about cost-benefit analysis that pharmacists don't understand? *Maybe they understand it perfectly. Are you willing to consider that?* She's willing to consider a lot of things. But not that.

I'm Saying When

GRETTA RUBS eyeliner from under her eyes and combs her hair back with her fingers. With a baby wipe, she cleans her hands and armpits. "PTA, remember that," her grandma has said. "A good pussy-tits-and-armpits bath is an important part of being on the road."

She puts Vaseline on her lips, and still she is not ready to go into the hostel. She has a history with this place that is less than pleasant. *An incidental backdrop.* It is not the youth hostel, she realizes, but more of her fucked-up *vitae*. Lacking in life experience, Gretta is not.

KeepOut.doc

```
I fucked around before the tequila man ever existed.
```

Gretta changes the name of *KeepOut* to *DescartesClassNotes* and shuts down. With a single act of documentation, she has entered a new level of secrecy.

She had been married for about a month and a half and had been giving Lance the silent treatment for about a week. When finally she spoke, Lance shattered a ceramic frog she'd made in the fifth grade then abandoned her to their apartment, which had already been broken into three times, twice with her in it. Monday went by. Tuesday, Wednesday, Thursday. With each day that passed, one longer than the previous, she grew angrier. She had no idea where he was.

She was baking the fourth batch of cookies since he'd left, the kind you roll in nuts then poke with your thumb to make a chocolate-chip nest. She reached for the cocoa and found an old friend's mother's number.

This friend and Gretta had gone to college together in Idaho—they'd met in biology. His name was Jeff. They started doing homework together after they realized they had grown up in the same city. They liked to complain about the same Utah things: hairspray, Jell-O casseroles, twelve-pack families, state-sponsored gerrymandering, ultra-right-wing politics in a church founded in a commune. ("Not much different," he liked to remind her, "from this shithole," meaning anywhere in southeastern Idaho.) Biology was his passion, he said, so for the next couple of years she wrote nature writing. She hadn't spent much time in nature, but she hoped to encyclopedically overcome her fear of it. Every word she wrote—on the biter monkey, the scaled gnopthia, the rain forests of Zaire—she wrote for him. She wrote of enraptured trees, heaving elk, quivering bodies of water. "Do you think I'll ever be as good as David Quammen?" she'd ask him. "Sure," he'd say. "Maybe." But Jeff was married—in love with his wife, no less—so nothing came of it.

After he graduated, he moved to Salt Lake to work as an accountant for his dad. He called her from a pay phone not long after he got there and asked her to meet him in Moab on the first of July, at this very hostel, the Lazy Lizard. His love for his wife, he said, had waned. She agreed, though questioned why they couldn't drive down together. "That's neither here nor there," he said. She still had a crush on him, so she didn't challenge his response.

He never showed up at the hostel. Apparently, he moved to Bozeman, Montana, at the end of June so his wife could be with her family. But it had been a long lonely while since he'd stood her up at the hostel, and besides, she had carried that ceramic frog around for so many years. She liked her life better before Lance could bust her things against a wall—before he'd entered her life only to leave it periodically. *Pneumatic nomadic. Pneumonic asthmatic. Numeric.... It doesn't mean anything. It doesn't mean anything. It doesn't mean anything—*

She called Jeff's mother's place. He was living at home in Salt Lake again. He said he had left his wife in Montana with a grocery clerk. Gretta said she needed company. He made it over to her apartment fast—before she'd tossed the last cookie in the bowl of nuts and filled it with chocolate chips. She put the cookies in the oven, set the timer for eight minutes, and came on to him hard. When the buzzer rang, she was sprawled out on the couch, half-naked, horrified, without climax, without so much as a kiss or a kind word. Jeff had already come. Gretta could see his wife's interest in the grocery clerk—in any clerk. Jeff left. Gretta never told him about Lance, and she never told Lance about Jeff. Still, it complicates the tongue-lashing she plans to give her husband.

~ Two Rapids Hotel ~

Fun for the whole famly!

Dear James,

Seriously, even IF Lance never came home—or IF I never took him back—how the hell would this work? Of course I don't think you're a kid, but you are what? Six, seven years younger than me? And your mother would still hate me. Your sister would still hate me. Lance would hate us both, and maybe your beloved Darrel would too. My kids would be confused. And I would still be, after all, me.

Love, Gretta

Her feet, she sees, are turned inward, toes curled. The flashbacks begin, each lasting no longer than the flick of a lighter: traces of dreams, of events that never took place, echoes of the current moment, of the woman sitting near. Part of her wants to see clearly; most of her just wants it all to go away. She closes her eyes and waits.

What does she want with me? The burning is almost unbearable—it's her whole body, as if blanketed by dry ice. The sinking feeling is soon overwhelmed by her presence. The woman. *Breathe two, three....* Who stands at the top of a tube. *Exhale two, three, four....* Who is angry. *Not angry.* Who wants something from her. She was here, parked at the hostel. In this truck, in this moment. She was already here. Gretta tries to look at her face, but it's as if Vaseline is smudged over her eyes. Part of her wants to listen; most of her just wants to die, until the burning breaks down to nausea and she knows the wave is passing. She waits.

When her breathing resumes autopilot and she becomes less dizzy, Gretta is ready. She tears up the note she wrote to James. She stuffs the quilt and a few clothes into her pack but leaves the suitcase in the pickup. It's a dumb case anyway—hard, blue, oddly sized, with an obnoxious alligator texture.

She drops her pack on the little dirt path in front of the hostel. A couple of men about her age sit at the picnic table outside the front door and gesture toward her with red plastic cups. They mutter to one another. Austrian or German, maybe. Definitely not American. She pretends she isn't interested.

She checks out the bulletin board. "Going to Colorado Springs, will pay half gas." And, "Going to San Francisco, need rider." She wishes—

You have kids to take care of, you careless fuck.

"Nine dollars," the man at the front desk says. It costs only two dollars more than it did the last time she was here a decade ago. She can still sleep here for less than the cost of a fifth.

She finds an empty bed and sets her pack, quilt, and laptop on the bottom bunk. Across the room is the bed she lay in over a decade ago—single, lonely, waiting to have sex with a married man and a newly fit diaphragm. She wonders whether she really thought she'd fuck in a dorm room—on a bunk bed, no less. She guesses they would have gone for a drive. The hostel has private rooms now, but she doesn't remember seeing them then. Maybe this logistical difficulty was the idea.

She doesn't know what to do about the kids. She is afraid of what Jackie might say about missing her date. She rifles through her pack for her phone. She is hoping to be inspired.

Do You Want to Save Changes?

"UTAH IS the dirtiest place I've ever been," says Peter, passing Gretta's bottle of magic sand to Stefan.

"It is," says Stefan. "Don't you think?" he asks Gretta. He pours some of the terracotta-colored sand into his palm, watches it drift aside with a breeze, then caps the bottle and gives it back to Gretta. An old man wearing biking gear comes out of the hostel; he nods at the three of them as he walks past. It seems he has no bike. *Youth hostel,* Gretta notes with relief, does not necessarily mean *hostel of youth.*

"My babysitter hates me," Gretta says, raising the bottle of sand to inspect it. She pours some into her own hand and recaps it, puts it in the center of the table. She would prefer a bottle of gin to the sand. "You guys know where Moab's liquor store is?" she asks.

"We bought the bourbon in Provo," says Stefan.

Stefan laughs at something Peter says; Gretta understood only the English of "state liquor store."

Peter grows more serious, looks at Gretta as if sizing her up. "The air from Salt Lake to Provo is dirty, all smog. I could not breathe there. Off to the side of the road in all of Utah is litter, like you're sending your garbage beside the highway."

"Yes," answers Stefan.

"No one lives like this anymore. Everyone in the Western world knows better. This is"— Peter gestures around them— "it's the Dark Ages."

It is getting dark. "That's right," Gretta says. "It's a potpie existence."

Abandonment. She is shocked anew each time she thinks of it. Her mother said it right in front of the kids. She is not abandoning them. She is retrieving their dad.

"They don't want to talk to you," her mom said when she called. "They probably don't trust you. Who would? You haven't spoken to them in over a week."

Gretta said she didn't believe her: she was sure the kids would want to talk to her. She tried to argue that they still seemed to trust their dad, and he really did abandon them. "Don't I deserve the same leeway?" she asked.

"Of course not—you're the mother. They can't talk regardless. They're getting ready for a birthday party. They're supposed to be there already. Alice is throwing a party for the twins at the Pizza Hut."

Gretta told her mom she was bitter and spiteful. "If I'm so spiteful," she answered, "why am I here taking care of your kids while you're out gallivanting around? Why am I always the first one to help you out of a crisis and the last one to be thanked for it?"

Her mother was right. Gretta can admit it now that she's had time to cool off. The woman bought Tulip and Braden meds if Gretta was broke; she watched the kids when she had to work weekends or simply fall apart in private; she paid for a new transmission for the pickup when Lance could not be reached. Gretta wishes she had bought her mom the clay plates that went with the salad bowl. She could either deliver them with gratitude or hurl them at her.

She could hear Braden crying in the background and Tulip yelling at him. "What's wrong with Braden?"

"Do you have to ask? This is a clear-cut case of abandonment we've got here. You've abandoned your own flesh and blood! You're going to end up right back in the hospital, sure as hell. You mark my words. Don't think I'm going to save you this time around."

Hurl. Gretta will pay interminably for her mother's favor. Her mom picked the kids up from Jackie on Friday afternoon. She must not have heard about the tequila man's tow-truck message, or she would have drilled Gretta about that. She seemed simply to accept that her daughter had gone missing.

"No!" Gretta yells now, but it comes out as "Uhn." Stefan and Peter are each holding a piece of the whistle. Gretta realizes she must have pulled the bandana out. She is sinking with the feeling that she's done something terrible. She told Lance she couldn't be trusted with sacred objects. He didn't believe her. "Put it back," she says. *Her voice cracks, rends, divides, revealing the crevice.*

"What is it?" Peter asks.

"Doesn't matter, put it back."

"Not until you tell me what it is." He sniffs it. He flicks it with his finger. He passes half of it to Stefan.

"A bone, I think," Stefan says. "Some kind of bone."

"Please give it to me. . . ."

"What, you mean this?" Peter says, tapping the whistle on the table.

"It's important. It's a whistle." Peter and Stefan blow on the pieces—she has said too much. "It's sacred," she says.

"Sacred?" Stefan pulls an electronic dictionary out of his breast pocket. He and Peter confer in German and then they laugh. They laugh until their eyes water. "Why do you care for sacred? 'I'm a woman without a god—I lost my passport in Limbo.' You said it yourself," says Stefan, grinning.

"You did," says Peter. "That's exactly what you said. And also: 'Now I'll have to fuck Dante too. Fuck him and all those—*was*?"

"Those miserable bees," says Stefan.

"Yes. Fuck the miserable bees." Peter laughs. "We did not expect you in Utah."

"Yeah, well, no atheists in foxholes."

"And you are in the foxhole?" Stefan asks.

"Or, 'Do unto others what they desperately need you to do'—she said that also," says Peter.

"I could make a necklace. Maybe a bracelet?" Peter says to Stefan.

Gretta reaches for his hand but he pulls it away. *Don't you dare cry.* Her eyes burn and her head spins on a gravel road. *I won't cry. I won't.*

"What's wrong with you? We make jokes," Peter says.

I've violated something. The thought does not induce a strategy. She doesn't know what would.

"We didn't mean to anger you." Stefan looks regretful and tosses his half on the table. She snatches it up, along with the bandana.

Peter is clearly annoyed. "Hey, where is my bourbon?" he asks.

Gretta feels sick. *How about your bourbon?* she thinks. *It was good, as bourbon goes.* She nods toward the bottle at the side of her, lying between the two boards that make up the bench she sits on. Peter leaves the other half of the whistle on the table and motions for Stefan to leave with him. Stefan waves. Peter grumbles in English about Americans. Gretta is left knowing it's too late, checking her memory for consequences.

"No consequences," she says to the whistle, and to herself, *No consequences.*

"Do you have to ask? This is a clear-cut case of abandonment we've got here."

She has also been told, "There is no such thing as cold air; there is only the absence of heat." The heat of the afternoon sun gave her a headache, but here, alone in the small halo of the porch light in front of the hostel, she sits in an unbearable absence of heat.

Inside, she makes her way upstairs to the bathroom and locks the door. She stares at the mirror until her face stops making sense and reassembles itself into someone else's face. She reads DON'T WASTE WATER, posted above the soap dispenser. *Hot water on a chilled girl is hardly a waste.* She steps into the shower once the water is hot. The water streams down her back as she leans forward onto the fiberglass wall. *Don't you cry.*

She wishes she had a razor. She plans to convince her husband he's better off at home, yet her legs look like a chimp's. Part of their premarital agreement was that Lance couldn't harass her to shave her legs. He'd run his hand upward, against the lay of the hair. He said the thickness was due to the higher testosterone level in white women. That's how white women got feminism, he said. She argued that feminism was counter to testosterone. Still, she often wonders whether Tulip will grow knifelike leg hair like her own or peach fuzz like Sylvia's.

Lance has always refused to believe Gretta's claim to feminism. He believes feminists have a plot to divide the Indian people—they want to do away with the men and make the women hate them. "They want to destroy the balance of tradition," he said.

"So I'm not a feminist, then? Well, you're not an Indian," Gretta said. "Apple!" She was on the inside of a locked door, but that didn't help. The bathroom doorframe burst. *It* was *an old apartment building.* Lance has never raised a hand at her, but he always had a thing for drama—for breaking things to make a point. Sometimes it terrified her, but breakage meant she would get a good apology later, usually involving a nice dinner and a backrub, so it wasn't all bad.

Someone pounds on the bathroom door. She gets out, dries off each limb with great care. *If I'm going to be a regrettable American,* she thinks, *I might as well go all out—get impudent.* She wants to yell, but nothing emerges. She dresses slowly, cleans her toenails, starting with the piggy that went to the market. She cleans her fingernails in like order, refusing to even look at the door that's getting a pounding, as if she is unwilling or unable to break up a ritual, a ceremony.

She doesn't just need a tool. She needs a ceremony, in addition to the ceremonious cleaning of toenails and fingernails. *Fishing?* Fishing is a ceremony of sorts. Fly fishing at least. *Burning something?* Burning anything besides fuel has got to count as ritual if she does it on a regular basis. *But what's the point?* And, *Well, Gretta, why does anyone need ritual? Comfort.*

That settles it. *Fuck ritual. To hell with ceremony. I don't need anything.* Self-soothe—a mother must teach her children to self-soothe, said all of the parenting books she read. Why should she be any different? *Because some ceremonies might be fun?*

Lance has told her that what is essential about a ceremony is that people express themselves. When the medicine man doctored the two of them because of the broken whistle, Lance was disappointed with

Gretta's lack of self-expression and said so. She couldn't say she was having fun, but she didn't cry out as he did.

Maybe she would have felt more expressive had she been told the range of things a medicine man might see in the coals. Could Erikson, for example, see her masturbating? Or how about the night when, at a high-school party, she made out with three different guys, thinking they were all the same guy? Or the time she bit the ear off her friend's chocolate Easter Bunny then replaced her sixteen Susan B. Anthonys with quarters, only to realize later that the girl had Hodgkin's lymphoma?

Or what about the nurse on the Greyhound? Or the Thai exchange student? Or the woman from Buffalo? Or how about when she told Lance that she suspected his sister of permanently borrowing her favorite cable-knit sweater, then when she found it in her bottom drawer, she didn't tell him?

Or the mess with the guy from Qatar, or the frat boy? Try a herd of them—a fucking montage of coked-up strangers. *Try—*

Some things must never be tried, never recalled. Violence may beget violence, and peace may beget peace, but memory, Gretta has learned, begets presence. Memory begets the vacuum.

She decided that if she thought of these things, these forbidden things, the medicine man would be more likely to pick up on them, so she tried to think of other things. Trilobites, for example. It wasn't working. She couldn't help thinking of all those memories that were her knowledge, her own *private* knowledge. She excused herself to the bathroom, made herself sick, but they didn't suggest she go to bed.

"That's what that thing does to you. That bad stuff is there and it will make you feel sick. That's what I'm here to help," Erikson said.

So she tried it again. *Elk and antelope—do they taste the same? Penguins—just how do they mate?*

"Sit up, like this. Your hands, like this."

Place settings—what is one to do with two spoons, two forks? If your napkin goes on your lap, what do you wipe your mouth with? The napkin on your lap or something separate? If you wipe something off your mouth, it'll get on your dress. If something has fallen on your lap, it might be smeared on your mouth—you couldn't inspect it, after all, under the table. If nothing is expected to fall in your lap or dribble down your mouth, why have a napkin? To show that one knows the napkin should go on the lap and not on the table?

But she was too curious about what Erikson was doing with the little rug, the things on the rug, the things…the things…*what things?* These things too are forbidden from speech. *These things too—*

In the end she thought, *Let him see me, if the coals are so good. Let him fix me. I'm not giving up anything for anybody.*

Then there was the bodily contact. Quiet or not, she was in some pain. Neck up or not, she was afraid. The only time anybody had been that close to her was during sex or rape. She didn't know whether to fall in love or scream, so she closed her eyes and waited for the pressure on her forehead to be over. Which, she reminds herself now, is not much different from her reaction to sex or rape.

"See?" Erikson said. "Bear bones." White flecks with spit. Gretta nodded yes. That's when he moved on to Lance.

First came the search and then the excavation, and that's when Lance expressed himself: he screamed.

The bedsprings squeal despite her efforts to be quiet. She considers whether her quilt would best be used to cushion her from the bedsprings or to keep her warm. For now, she turns down the hostel's blanket, folds her own in half, and lies down on it. She looks at her life and wonders how it happened. She's a heterosexually married woman—or something similar—with children, lying alone on a thinly blanketed bunk bed.

Someone begins to snore. Softly at first, then louder.

She reaches to the bottom of the bed for her pack and pulls out a flashlight. She pauses between movements, as every move she makes seems to echo in the room, but no one stirs. She feels around for her laptop, which has been juicing up under the bed. The cord won't quite reach around the bed frame, so she tugs it out. She tries to shush the speaker as the computer boots up. She looks around the room, which is now cast in the faint blue light. She waits for protest. She counts the mounds of sleepers—seven. The snoring gives her a sense of justification. She presses the dictionary open with her foot and holds the little flashlight between her teeth.

`WordsforLater.doc`

`Homosexuality:` `Of, relating to, or characterized by a tendency to direct sexual desire toward another of the same sex.`

Beth, short for Bethany. When she brought her home, her family assumed it was rape that "did it" to her. They blamed it on Qatar, they blamed it on the frat houses, on her university. They speculated that maybe she had been molested by her kindergarten teacher—"damned hippie," her mother had said. Maybe it was the chemical imbalance that was also the root of her depression. Perhaps it was "that goddamned HBO" her father had insisted they have. They urged her to go to a shrink to find out what was wrong with her so the problem could be repaired.

But what if (she wanted to tell them) it was the elasticity of Bethany's skin, or her hips—at times full and round, at times concave? No less compelling, though, were Lance's temples, which pulsed when he was excited, or the density of his forearms, or the soft grit in his voice. The long, smooth planes of his chest.

`TheLover.doc`

`It's nineteen-ninety-something. We are crouched`

"No, no, and no."

`Do you want to save changes to "TheLover"?`

Gretta shakes her head, clicks No.

`DescartesClassNotes.doc`

`It was nineteen-ninety-something. We were crouched,`

facing each other, in the back of the cab of his cousin's white pickup. Leonard was going ninety-five miles an hour. His girlfriend laughed about it. She called him a crazy Indian. I could barely hear them over the music—the White Fish Juniors, loud as can be. I was grateful because all I had been able to think about until the week before, when I met Lance, was Bethany. And now the drum was everywhere, everything, and the pain receded. I looked at Lance, who was holding his knees like I was. He was so beautiful—effusive as a puppy, graceful as a spider. I was hot and buzzing and ready to drag him to bed. But he seemed happy to be where he was. I reached my hand out and he took it. The pain was weightless in his hand. He smiled, and that's what I wanted. I wanted to become a part of such happiness.

Then:

Do you want to save changes to "DescartesClassNotes"?

"Sure."

A throat is cleared. "Sorry," Gretta whispers. But what is the tapping of keys compared to obnoxiously loud snoring?

WordsforLater.doc

Tendency: Direction or approach toward a place, object, effect, or limit. A proneness to a particular kind of thought or action. The purposeful trend of something written or said: AIM. Deliberate but indirect advocacy.

AIM. *American Indian Movement. Take aim. Aim higher.* She aspires to deliberateness, but she's not convinced she's capable of it.

WordsforLater.doc

Homoscedacity: The property of having equal statistical variances.

"Could you turn that off, please?" the throat-clearer asks, irritated. Gretta shuts down, softly snaps her laptop shut, and slides it under the bed. *Where is your impudence now?* she thinks, and, *I've had my daily share.*

She tries to find a comfortable spot on the bed, but every time she turns, the bed squeaks. She settles into her kerchief of a blanket and lies still, listening to the sounds of sleepers, giving up on her own sleep. If she were wealthy, she'd donate heavy blankets and nice soft pillows to the hostel; then the place would be perfect. People like her didn't remember to bring a sleeping bag or pillow with them, but people like her needed the anonymous social intimacy and generosity of hostels, maybe even more than the internationals with their mummy bags needed them.

If the bed will not bring her comfort, even cushioned by the quilt, the quilt might as well keep her warm. She scoots under it.

The young woman in the bunk above her moans softly, and the bed begins ever-so-slightly to shake, or perhaps Gretta is imagining it. She moans again, but the moaning is drowned out by someone else's snoring. Gretta decides the woman must be dreaming. Surely no one would masturbate in a room full of people. The woman falls silent. Gretta touches the bottom of the top bunk, where the mattress bulges through the slats. She wonders if a part of James enjoys Mr. Cox's semiprivate interludes—if they are contagious, if they make him miss sex. Who had James had sex with? She can think of no one. She's never thought of asking, and he's never offered the information. He's never told her about a girlfriend, even. *He can't be a virgin.* If he's having sex, he's certainly not a braggart. If he's not, what could he possibly have against Cox?

If he were a virgin, and things didn't work out with Lance, they could have good old-fashioned unprotected sex. *Unless—*

Could she get STDs from oral sex? *You should know these things!* If she contracted something from the tequila man, she'd be morally obligated to tell Lance about it before they had sex. That wouldn't go over well. *"You what? With a hitchhiker?"*

She'd just have to get tested first. "Maybe we shouldn't have sex for a couple of weeks," she could suggest. "Let's clear our heads, talk about things first." How would a counselor say it? "Let's wait until we're emotionally ready to begin the healing process."

She begins to take her laptop out again, to Google *oral sex* and *STD*, but decides she doesn't want to know—not until she's had a good six hours of sleep, at least. *Anyway, he aimed high, didn't he?* And she *had* planned to make Lance get tested first.

The bed begins to shake again—just a bit, then faster. What would her bunkmate's sock read? *Montagne? Schmidt? Gonzales? Smith?* The shaking stops; the woman breathes deeply, as if stepping outside to take a breath of fresh air.

Gretta considers following suit but is struck by an image of another woman's legs wrapped behind Lance's back. He grinds against her slowly, purposefully. Nothing unintentional or accidental about thrusting your ass around. Therein lies the drawback to being a man, she decides. You can't lie waiting for it all to be over. You can't disown participation afterward, or dull your sense of complicity to unrecognizable proportions. *You can't check yourself in—*

She wonders who she'd be, had she not the option of playing the passive observer of events that were, arguably or not, beyond her control.

As a Matter of Spite

WHEN GRETTA sees the sign (REPENT, SINNERS! THE END GROWS NEAR AND GOD SHALL HAVE HIS VENGENCE!) nailed to a post in front of a trailer house just outside of Taylor's Creek, she knows exactly what her grandmother spoke of. The white wooden board with painted red letters is uncomfortably familiar. She pulls over and checks behind her seat—an empty jar smelling of apricots. She could check for new photos on her phone, but decides knowledge might, at this point, hurt rather than help. She drives on slowly, her window half rolled down.

The town is eerily quiet, with not a dog in sight. A gas station stands boarded up. A cannery, boarded up. A small general store, boarded up. Makeshift ranch homes and trailer houses are surrounded by heaps of junk cars, rusting farm equipment, and miscellaneous objects. Clothes hang on clotheslines. Flags and crosses and evangelical quotations hang in nearly every window, stand posted in every yard; Gretta wonders how she found herself in the Bible Belt in the big toe of Colorado. She thought the Four Corners area was reserved for, at the most exotic, polygamists. She considers Nancy of Hiawatha. She'd sooner go to the Mormon church with Nancy on the Sunday of the month when women cry and men boast of being humble as step outside the pickup here. And her grandmother said what? *You demanded proof of God's word.* That she approached someone's home? *You asked whether immaculate conception meant God had sex with Mary or the sperm was spirited into her.* That she accepted apricots? *They could have been poisoned, for the way you spoke to the woman of the house, and yes, you ate them. Every last one.*

Whose voice was this voice of authority? Who here was the observer? *Another kind of hallucination?*

"What are the chances I have schizophrenia?" she asked her neurologist once.

"You hear the voices outside your head or inside?" he asked her.

"Inside."

"Slim."

Her nurse practitioner said the same, as did a counselor for an eight-hundred hotline. Her memory, then, had a voice of its own.

She does like apricots. Now that she thinks about it, she sees a face—freckled, not so old, furrowed brow. A woman holds out a Bible and says something mean—Gretta can't remember what. Maybe it wasn't even mean; maybe it was just a quote from the Bible.

"Maybe it's the voice of God." That's what a priest told her when she went to see what a confessional booth was like. But when she gave the priest an idea of the kinds of things her brain said to her, he changed his mind.

Before Lance left, he requested a meeting with Erikson to see if he might be able to "cure" her—maybe he could make the seizures go away or resolve other "mental issues." Maybe the medicine man could help their marriage, which translated to her as his hope that Erikson could make her stop drinking. Sylvia joined them, as she'd been having chronic headaches.

Lance got the usual diagnosis: someone is jealous, someone is trying to witch you, et cetera. But Gretta got words that still disturb: "I can help you but only if you open up and take it in a good way. If you can't think about God or the Creator, think of all those things, those people, your childrens, your mom, your dad—all those things you love. Or that pretty landscape or that hummingbird, you know. That feeling you get then, when you see those things—that is your spirituality. That is your God. Think like that."

"I don't know what you mean." But Gretta knew exactly what he meant—he gave her the same inadequate message she'd gotten at AA.

Sylvia said, “Basically he’s saying that spirituality as a matter of spite is not going to help you. When you think of that higher power, you have to think of good things. You know?” Sylvia must have been thinking of good things, because the tone of her voice had not a single sigh of derision in it. She looked encouragingly at Gretta, even.

Erikson continued: “Then use that spirituality to live in a good way and to be a good wife to your husband.” She’d been so annoyed by the sheer semantics of that last comment that she didn’t admit until later, in private, that he had also told Lance to be a good husband to his wife.

Gretta had taken her medicine that night, but wishes she could have asked a question that might have allowed her to digest his advice: *Yes, but if God is a forest and the forest is cleared, what then? If God is the feeling I get with the people I love and they leave me, to whom do I pray?*

There’s not much to clear in the desert. No one to grant or withdraw love on a dirt road in the desert. “Dear desert. Oh, desert. Take pity on me,” she whispers. *Shit.* Tomorrow she will have to Google *prayer* and see what she comes up with.

Keeping It Out

"THERE IS a contrast in the sky that can't be explained by her presence in a foreign nation. The sun is lit up crimson in the east, the clouds are brass-gold-green in the west, they move so fast. She has never seen such fast-moving clouds."

She gets out of the truck. Her narrative appears in her mind letter by letter, as if on a concave screen. The inevitability of letter-to-word-to-sentence, of setting-to-climax-to-resolution, seduces and suffocates, for the setting has set, and any one of the many possible climaxes couldn't possibly render finality. The narrative persists regardless.

"She looks for herself in the sky and can't imagine where she might fall. She is somewhere in the middle, or on top where she can't be seen, or she is on the wooden steps leading to the trailer house."

The steps creak; there is no going around them. "Little doggie?" There are cans with nails in them. The nails are separated by size and all are rusting on the wooden steps. They grow larger, smaller, larger, smaller. The offensive sky marbleizes the sparkly clean aluminum siding of the trailer house. The distraction offers nothing in the form of consolation.

"Come here," she could say. "You might never see a sky like this again." But the vacuous air offers nothing in the form of reconciliation. A laugh begins but it rolls into a deep shiver. Her tongue is fat and dry. She bites it, tastes blood but feels little.

Six cars are parked in the driveway—among them, hers. *The famly car,* she thinks. "It is as if the cars are parked at a drive-in theater, fixed in a photograph of a drive-in theater.

"That's Lance on the screen, pulling her into the street behind the bar. The street is narrow, the graffiti is scarce, the shadows of doors are inviting. And the buildings! They. Are. So. Tall.

"What's at the end? she says. *I don't know,* he says. *I've never been golden in my life.* They lean together and walk on the pavement, like mud. She wants to see the end."

"Hello?" says the phone.

"They lean together, his skin so smooth, they hit a loading dock. She unbuttons his shirt. They are sweaty and reeking of alcohol and smoke. She leans into him. He is so warm, she represents nothing. His hand slides up her thigh and between her legs, but it is as if it is a photocopy of a hand on a photocopy of a thigh."

"Who is this?"

"For him it is the end of drinking. For her it is the middle."

"I think it's for you. I think it's her.... I can't tell what she's saying."

She has a sickness, but nothing comes out. "She considers rapping on the door. I'm not going in there, she thinks with posterity, austerity, temerity. Posterior. Vortex."

It is not that she has been drinking, nor that she is thinking aloud to a capsule of Arizona air. It is not that she is a child-abandoner or the self-hatred tracing words on her skin: *Go A-way. Stay A-way.* It is that outside the trailer park there is an open space that spreads for miles and miles and she is stumbling somewhere in the middle.

"She's blowing around in the night sky—will she freeze, will she die? Will she unbutton her blouse? She's on a porch and she's wearing an ugly smelly shirt. It's got something on it."

"Wait! Don't open the door!"

She touches a wet spot on her shirt. She stumbles back to the truck. She sits in the cab, looking for a voice of reason to tell her what to do. She hears only dizziness.

She backs up the truck, feels a thump, and speeds away. *No more foxes.* She drives for what seems like ages.

She is nauseous and tired. So tired, her body is in total agreement: she wants only to sleep. The darkening sky concurs. There is a howling—loud, clear, whirling around and alongside her. She pulls over, rolls down the window. The howling bounces off the heavy lining of earth and sky. She wants to jump out of the truck, call on the coyotes, tell them to fuck off with their straight pubic hair, but suddenly she hears nothing. She feels nothing. The desert is as hollow as a clean Mason jar. The desert calls her inside. Maybe it is the fox who calls. She rolls up her window, because if she can't call it on, then she must keep it out. *If I had kept it out,* she thinks, *kept it out all along—*

"There she was: sick, puking, dragging." The girl was charred, dismembered, and she dragged her through the forest. *They* dragged her through the forest, the wet forest, the forest of foot rot, the forest of gun smoke, smoldering leaves, irreconcilable senses—that is the beauty of the wet trees and the light show above, the horror of young infantrymen.

"Or she was dragged astray, dragged through the forest, charred, dismembered, deteriorating, wondering who was dragging her and what for—why the women didn't just let her go, let her gravitate beneath—"

Or she awoke in a park on a Sunday morning unearthed, feeling that someone had jammed a knife inside her and slit her open, vagina to belly. "There she was: sick, puking, dragging." There had been a change, she could feel it, and it wasn't just the pain. She found her way home, then stood in front of a mirror looking for proof, looking for entrails. She found nothing, nothing but a couple of abrasions—abrasion of thigh, abrasion of throat, burning of pelvis. They would be gone by the next business day. She couldn't afford to go into an emergency room on a weekend. She'd never be able to pay it off. She was barely able to pay for her books, for food, for rent. In fact, she hadn't paid rent and she stole or dated for half of the food she ate. She would have to wait for her doctor, the weekday doctor, and beg him to mark the consultation as brief. But by then it'd be no good, because she wasn't going to let the semen rot inside her for two days. She had counted—day thirteen of her cycle. In two days' time, she could very well be pregnant, by god knows which one of them, and it wouldn't be the morning after. *Does it have to be the morning after?* She had never heard of a morning-after-morning-after-night pill. And anyway, she could not pay nor tolerate the law laying her out, laying her flat. She had no proof of nonconsent, no irrefutable proof of a failed getaway, no good reason for being the only girl at the party, and by the time she finished showering, she'd surely have released herself of the awful evidence. *Wouldn't I have?* She'd been tanked—drunk still in the morning. That, in itself, ruled out her rights—at least in the state of Idaho. Idaho—*"It's safe here."* For Lance, maybe. For women, it was a free-for-all.

It was too much. She gave up, puking, dragging. Ultimately she cracked open her geology book and took license with the names of rock formations. Ultimately she threw the book against the wall and turned on the tube and watched *Hamburger Hill* for the third time that week. Ultimately she felt like hamburger, felt as though she had been ground and eaten, and she had been. She had been. It turned out that the abrasions she couldn't bring herself to touch required stitches. Seven stitches, stitched later by the weekday doctor who stitched disdain into her—unhappy, he said, with girls the likes of her. If it was nonconsensual, why hadn't she reported it? If it was *not* nonconsensual, why couldn't she just keep her legs shut, or, at this point, her mouth? "Why make excuses for what you must *ultimately* take responsibility?" Had this happened to her before? he wondered. She wasn't about to arm him with an answer. He concluded for her with a nod. Then he loaded her up with antibiotics and cold packs for the infection that had taken hold over the weekend. She couldn't remember the details—she blacked out, she could have said. There were so many, she could have said. But nothing could be done about the hamburger. It would have to be eaten or there it would rot and the stench would drive people away—the doctor, for instance. Already the stench was driving people away. It was driving her away.

Endoscopic fuckers.

WordsforLater.doc

Endoscope: An instrument with which the interior of a hollow organ (as the rectum) may be visualized.

Endothermic: Characterized by or formed with absorption of heat.

"Endothermic fuckers, all," she says.

Emulsion: A mixture of mutually insoluble liquids in which one is dispersed in droplets throughout the other: a light-sensitive coating on photographic film or paper.

She and her tendencies— *No, pronenesses! No pronenesses!*

Prone: Bent forward, tending; akin to. Having a tendency or inclination: being likely. Having the front or ventral surface downward. Lying flat or prostrate.

She and her hang-ups. She and her crassness, her pronenesses. She listens for a voice of comfort. She requests a voice of comfort. She submits, *Dear God, give me comfort,* but she feels numb. She feels trembling, puking, pissing.

Fuck AA and fuck the higher power. I submit nothing, I will never submit, not a damned thing. She feels the dirty earth rotting her from the inside out, the caked blood and the napalm. She smells the smoke—burnt hair, burnt nails, burning grasshoppers. She feels mistaken.

Dear God, make it stop. It doesn't stop. It's a train. And her skin, it burns. The women mutter unintelligibly. They taunt her periphery with their cause. Some indiscernible, relentless cause. And all the while she goes on thinking, living, pushing as if they weren't there. She ignores them, sometimes for months at a time. But times like these, she looks right at them. She can see their mouths move. They seize the chance, front and center. They drag her over the leaves to the netherside of the DMZ. The woman directs.

The nausea, the doubt, the physiology—clitoris, ear wax; speech, bile. She doesn't get it. *It's only moving.* And the sanity, it comes in waves. It comes in jellies. It's—*Jesus, I don't feel right.* Every movement generates heat, and generation is something she doesn't want to do. She wants to hold it close, but not too close. Words are too much. Words are too little. She wants something more. She wants to see it all, as if in crystal, but her eyes are plump as grapes and swelling still. She wants grammar. She wants syntax. She wants to hear the whole bloody story, but she can't bear to tell it.

She has gone too far. Her follicles tickle and torment relentlessly. There is a pounding at her window. *A pounding.*

"Could you roll down the window? Miss?"

She rolls down the window an inch, staring intently at the steering wheel. "She is in a bizarre Hillerman novel in which there is a white girl."

"I said, could you roll down the window, please? All the way down?"

"There is a man, he asks for papers-identification-proof of insurance. The window is not a window but a wall that refuses to roll down. The girl is asked to remove herself from the vehicle."

"Excuse me?"

"Seventy-two hours."

"Seventy-two hours to what, ma'am?"

"RU-486. She learns later it's good for seventy-two hours. Or more." She stares out the window. She finds it silent in the vacuum. The ceiling no longer calls to her. She feels only the debris, is the debris, the sediment. To begin, to climax, to conclude…to learn, to grow, to regress…tomorrow, yesterday, her coat closet, a bowl of cereal—sameness prevails in the vacuum, in no particular order, along no particular arc. It is possible she has set anchor in her Orient. Finally. Irreversibly. Even reluctance loses sight of its homeland. The steering wheel is covered in lamb's wool. *Lucky for me,* she thinks. Lance had insisted. She lays her head on the soft wool.

Words for Later

She wakes to noise. There is the blue and the black, and the fluorescent lights between. The noise recedes and the darkness returns, a cavern. The woman is central. She is mostly buried, though traces of her have been unearthed. It is Gretta's duty to pay homage to her corpse. She is horrified. She doesn't want to look. She is pushed, by what, she doesn't know—compelled to touch the dust she is becoming. She reaches out, but her body shakes, and the hand draws back. The granules and chips and hair of grayness melt her eyes. There is no window separating herself from this place, only a faint light that seems to precede it. The grayness starts at the fingertips, reaches up the trembling arm, disperses to vital organs until she becomes a part of the discolor. The air is so dry, her nose cracks, bleeds. She tries to run but there are so many graves, so many gravestones. She looks to Lance and the children for comfort but knows this is the one place they will never be: living Navajo among the dead.

She stumbles on the granules and chips of legs, dodging bones, dodging stones, ducking and trying to protect her head with her hands from the sharp protrusions above. But the corpses, they're everywhere, and with each step more graves are unsettled. They unleash clouds of age and mold. She doesn't want to look, but with her eyes dripping like wax, she can't help but see. The death, the violence, the aggravation. The discontentment rubs at her, rubs the granules and chips of her hips, her abdomen. Rubs at her chest, her shoulders, her arms. *This is who I am,* she thinks. *This is who I might always be.* She reaches up, touches the rocky skin of the cave. She tastes only blood. She searches for a hole—a hole in the bag from which she might emerge.

She pulls herself up, feet swiping for footholds. She emerges, rests at the top. She is re-embodied. And the body, it aches. The blood runs clearer—clear, now. A bird of prey shrieks—hawk or eagle, she doesn't know. She looks for the bird but finds instead that she has emerged into another burial ground. Uninhabited but marked by previous beings. With petroglyphs, with salt. *This is not your house.* With stone tools and corn. With gourds and bowls. *You don't belong here.*

Suddenly she is surrounded by the living—her father, her mother, her brother. "We can't stay," she whispers. "You can't touch those things. Leave them be."

"Touch what, honey?"

She looks for the hole in the skin of the sky, but finds herself on a ledge of crumbling sandstone. The canyon below is so deep, she can't make out the bottom. The ledge, so narrow. It's a vast emptiness growing nearer. She shouts to her mother, "Don't plug it in! There'll be dirt and hair all over the place." But when she turns around, she sees that she is alone again. She is dizzy. Her ass tingles, her toes curl. She wants to vomit, but—*If I move... if I move...*

"You think she's okay? Maybe we should just call him."

It's death that she wants and death that she fears. It's the long teeth-aching fall. She can't bring herself to jump, but gravity is getting the best of her. Gravity pulls her deep into the Mason jar. She closes her eyes and hears the lid screw shut. "She's out again."

The sheets smell clean but feel gritty. Braden has been eating in her bed. She can't get up. She can't move. The air presses down on her. She listens to the clicks and groans of the old house. They prefer her to stay in bed. They sedate her.

Lance wanders around the room, wondering what he has forgotten. His hair has been cut short and his waist and arms seem to have grown heavier.

"You're my piece of bread," she explains.

He looks at her but does not seem to see her. "Huh?"

"When the cookies go hard. When I left out the cookies."

He insists he put a tape measure in the bottom drawer of the dresser. The dresser presses down on her. Soon she will be unable to breathe. She must say what she has to say in order to say it right.

"You put the cookies in a bag with the bread and by morning they're soft again."

"You had to have moved it. Think. Think."

What would I want with a tape measure? she thinks. *It hasn't been given to me.*

He is standing over her. The dresser dissipates, becomes an immovable object behind him, a dresser half-covered with bottles of perfume and cat figurines. A tapestry and a rug on the wall, side-by-side.

She looks around. She's in Angela's room, in the trailer house—no Braden, no bread crumbs, no bread.

Much sun comes through the window. She tries to put together what Lance is saying but can't quite, until he says, "…words for later."

Her vessels contract. She wakes and stares at the ceiling a moment; the room slowly comes to a standstill. "Did you go through my files?"

"Should I have?"

Her notes, her letters to James…. *Recent Documents.* She tries to gather her thoughts. "Did you?"

He laughs. "Things are different around here. Otherwise, you'd be in jail still," he says. "Where are the kids?" It is possible he didn't read them; otherwise she'd be in jail—*still?*

"The kids. God, my head."

"The kids?"

"The kids are with Jackie."

"I called your mother." He always calls the mother. Everyone, it seems, calls the mother. "She says she has them."

The smug tone of his voice hurts her head. "Oh. Yeah." She wishes she had orange juice.

"You think you need to…you know, go back?" He waits. "To the hospital, I mean?"

"I went to the hospital?"

"Not last night. The *state* hospital—at the U."

She gathers her thoughts, and with them an ache and an understanding. "Fuck you, Lance."

He rubs his head, sighs at length. "You should be with the kids," he says.

"*You* should be with the kids."

He lies down beside her on the fresh-smelling bedding and holds her. It is his wide warm hands that she loves. The near hairlessness of his arms. He kisses the back of her head, her hair, and she is reminded of the tequila man.

"I'm sorry," she says.

"For what?"

"For smelling like this."

"It's not that bad. We put you in the shower last night. As for your breath—well, we sprayed your mouth with that stuff."

"Where's Angela?"

"Visiting a friend." The bed creaks as he unhinges himself from her and rolls off the bed.

"Did you miss me?" she asks.

"I did," he says. He pulls on a T-shirt. "Come on."

"Get my pants, please."

"No one's home. It's okay."

"Did you know the Mormons believe your skin is dark because you're cursed?" she asks as she follows him into the kitchen, tugging her shirt down to her thighs.

"Yeah, I know."

"And then when you're converted—" He gives her a sharp look. "I mean, according to *them*...when the Native Americans convert, they will turn light again or something." He doesn't respond. "I mean, I'm sure no one really believes it anymore. Except the dumb ones."

He pours Gretta a bowl of Pops with whole milk, her favorite. "Not everyone has to be full-on converted and baptized to get lighter. The

Navajo people 'are fast becoming a white and delightsome people.' You know who said that? President Spencer Kimball." He adds, in a mocking voice, "'The Indian children in the home-placement program in Utah are often lighter than their brothers and sisters in the hogans on the reservation.' Lucky I wasn't adopted by Mormons, huh? I'd lose my year-round tan."

"Huh…that's fucked up. So why does Sylvia…?"

"Why does Sylvia do anything?"

"Just for the record, *I* don't think you're cursed by God."

He laughs. "You don't believe in God."

"Yeah, well."

"Thanks. Just for the record." He rummages through the pocket of his coat, which is hung on the back of a chair. "See?" he says. He sets a bag of ribbon candy on the table. "I went shopping for you. Sorry, no bread. I tried to find your pills, but I couldn't see them anywhere. How you feeling this morning?"

Her Zoloft had to be in the pickup when he looked. She checks her pockets—nothing. She looks around for her keys, her pack, her jacket. Nothing looks like hers. "Where did you put my keys?"

"I didn't put your keys anywhere. You thinking of leaving?"

"Maybe," she says.

"Can you answer my question first?"

She walks outside but there is no pickup. She feels a little silly. She sits at the kitchen table to steady her head. *Was it towed? Could I have wrecked it?* She's pretty sure she would remember that. *It would've hurt, wouldn't it have?* There would likely be a hospital involved. The pickup could be at the side of the road somewhere. She won't know how to get there. She'll have to ask someone to take her there. She'll have to ask Lance or—*shit!*—Angela.

Lance stands in the doorway. "Blowing around in the night sky, are we? Will she starve? Will she freeze? Will she…," he says, smiling nervously, staring at her with a big chin nevertheless—he is the winner: "…unbutton her blouse?"

"What?" She would like to feel as though, for once, she is in control of herself and she can politely ask the world to cooperate with her. She doesn't know where to start.

"You were narrating again," he says.

She pushes past him. He follows her into the kitchen.

"When?" Her face is hot. Her hair feels greasy and she's not even touching it.

"You called. Last night."

"That call wasn't meant for you."

"No? Who was it meant for?"

"I didn't mean to call anyone."

"You know, a person should have to earn the right to drive a car. A person should have to prove himself. You—you shouldn't even have a license," he says. "On many counts." An attempt at funniness is in his voice but she is certain he's serious, and maybe afraid. Definitely angry.

He rubs the back of his head. "How can I leave the kids with you when you just—"

"That's right, how could you?" She wants to say more, to point out his error. Tell him he's cursed, he's getting lighter. Tell him he's a bad driver. Tell him she doesn't like powwows—she never has. Too many people are mean to her, petty. And he doesn't stick up for her. And the garbage disposal is broken, as is the dryer, the truck, the air-conditioner—*and he hasn't done a fucking thing about it!* And Braden got on a bike for the first time, and who's to thank? *Not Lance!* And it's his fault she was given oral sex because… *Because damned if he was giving you anything.* She wants to feel like she knows something and her life will be easier because of it. She would like a sense of dignity, as when one buys cheese from the deli: "I want a pound and a half of that, please, and slice it thin." But there seems to be no way of asking, "Has my truck been impounded?" and "Will you give me the respect I deserve?" Not in the same moment.

State hospital. Who will bring her edible food? *Your mother?*

"Where is the truck?" she asks too loudly. She sounds like a goose. *Honk honk.*

"Don't you remember?"

She squeezes her head. She rubs her face and rubs her eyes almost out and still she is mad. She calls information. "I need the number of the police in Fort Defiance, Arizona, please." Lance hangs up the phone.

"Angela has it. She's going to town for a couple of hours. Believe me, you don't want the police to come back here."

Gretta punches the box of Pops and cereal flies everywhere. "You clean it up, asshole. I fucking hate you!"

She runs back to the bedroom with her arms flailing like a four-year-old's, the goose chasing her inside the room. *Don't cry.* She leans against the door and braces her leg against the dresser so he can't get in. Of course he gets in. He always gets in. *Am I a victim?* Her limbs feel drained and her heart is racing. She gives up and folds over on shag carpet, trying to catch her breath. *Do I like it?*

Spare me the anguish and the human suffering, will you?

He stands over her for a long time. His breath slows. She is angry still, but she doesn't have the energy for another performance, and the goose is completely out of hand. He lies down next to her on the bedroom floor. They lie motionless; she listens to an unseen clock. Her throat hurts, her head aches.

He strokes her arm, and she wonders how feeling alien has come to feel so familiar.

"What happened to Angela's dog?" she asks once the sob in her throat dissipates.

"He ran away," Lance says.

"Poor thing."

"You never liked him anyway."

"He bit me."

"What happened to the truck?" Lance asks.

"What do you mean?"

"It's all…dented…and scratched up and everything."

"Oh, that." First she pulled out in front of a minivan, then she left Tulip and Braden with her mom for a long weekend on a suggestion from her caseworker. Tulip was so angry, she scratched up the truck and the coffee table the day she got home. "Neighbor kids. They had a party. It got really wild…when the cops arrived, these strippers from Denmark…" She reaches back to touch his shoulder. "Just kidding. I did it. It needed a paint job anyway."

"Were you keeping up with the insurance?"

"Yes, but…I mean, it would be easier if you could help."

"I guess you don't know."

"Don't know what?"

"I paid for it two weeks ago. You didn't even notice, did you? I paid for the whole premium. Paid the utilities, too. You know they were going to shut the power off?"

"It's been hard."

"I know. I'm sorry." He brushes her hair back, then tickles her arm again, says, "You used to love me, didn't you?"

Once, during an argument, he'd pulled a quilt her grandma had made her from the closet. He made her take a look at the tiny hand stitches that made up every two-inch square of the blanket. "That's love," he challenged her. "We're not even close to that." She responded by pouting.

Her response today: "What makes you think I don't love you now?"

"Christ, Gretta. Why do you always have to ask stupid shit?" The tickling stops. He waits, maybe for an answer. "Why can't you just say you love me or you don't? Everything's like that with you. I want…I really want to see the kids…be at home with the kids, with you…but I can't take it. You can't say what you feel; you can't say what you think. I ask you something, and you answer with a question, or it's this…blank stare. A blank stare and a shrug."

"What do you want me to say?"

"Oh! See? One after another. And you're drinking all the time. You think I don't know, but I know. Do you have any idea how hard it is to stay sober? Maybe I shouldn't tell you this, but it's hard. Every day is one long fucking day for a good two years, and then it's still hard.

And there you are, right in the house, with your stupid stash that you think I don't know about, or trying to get me out to the bar with your stupid, fucking friends."

"Friend."

He's right, though, she does have questions—lots of them. But this time she really would like to concede an answer. What does she feel? She searches. *Affection? Repulsion? Fear?* She thinks very, very hard. She senses that this is the moment she is supposed to tell him that she loves him, that he should come home because she loves him, and she will quit drinking, and they will live happily ever after, as a *famly*. She might ask that he not break things. She might offer that she will be more tolerable. But the key words sound so disingenuous: *I love you*. Even if it's so. *How do I love him? What for?* She wants to offer substance, she wants to be convincing. She considers various avenues—ways of loving. One is blocked by her mother, another by her father, another by the man cut in fourths. Still another is blocked by his mother, his aunt, his sister. In another, Jeff, the frog. In one, another woman stands at the end of the street, her arms folded, waiting. Men. So many of them. So many avenues, so many barriers. *In what way can I love him? What's left?* She wants to deliver at least one good answer. She listens closely. Nothing comes.

"I missed you," she says.

He falls back, closes his eyes. "I missed you, too."

And Also It Goes Back to That Whistle

SHE FEELS around under the seat—they didn't confiscate her gin. Her camera is there. Her suitcase is in the back. She checks the glovebox—her books are there. But the dictionary—she is desperate for grounding—maybe the officer took it. Maybe it fell out. *Maybe you were dragged out of the truck.* The dictionary is gone—it isn't in the truck. Not anymore.

Her step is unruly. *No twitching.* She tries to carry herself as if nothing is the matter. *Stop biting your lip.* The trailer house is so small and dark, she can't quite see—that, and she can't quite breathe. The air is stagnant, hot, thick. She tries to focus on the conversation she has walked into, but the air is so dry she cannot breathe.

"That's what you think will fix everything? A psychologist?" And to Gretta, "Do you hear that? Lance thinks you need a psychologist," Angela says.

Gretta drops the keys on the counter, stares at Lance. Perhaps he took the dictionary.

Angela says, "You ever play those puzzle? You got a puzzle and it's missing one piece. You put it all together and you got one piece missing. It don't feel right. It don't feel finish. It could be one piece, it could be four. It still don't feel right. That's what that psychology does. It puts this piece and that together. But you won't find a psychologist who will tell you, 'I got all the missing piece right here.' That's not how it is for us. For people, you and me. Some people die, sometimes you might lose something. You forget. Like that. You can remember this or that or have another kid when your children dies. But you can't ever find all the piece. You want to be happy? To raise those children in a good way? You don't look at it like a puzzle. You don't go looking for all the piece. You ask for help. You need to pray. You forgot how to pray. That's why things are not good for you."

Gretta whispers to Lance, "Where is my dictionary? It wasn't in the truck. It wasn't there."

She tries to put his bewilderment into perspective. Lance couldn't possibly understand why she needs it—that the dictionary tells her how to do it, how to live, how to know what comes next. It speaks to her, and he does not—few do. Its availability is uncanny. Its sequence, fate. Inevitable. Until now. Now it's gone. Now someone will look at it, at the notes she has taken, the underlining, the highlighting, the dog-earing, the cross-references. They might make something of it. There might be questions. There might be suggestions, enforcements, reinforcements.

Maybe Angela took it. Angela—a thorn in Gretta's back. When Jackie was twelve, her father put a thorn in her bra to try to make her stand up straight. It didn't work; Jackie had scoliosis. *So it is with you.*

She wonders whether she has always felt this combustible and whether she'll feel such violence tomorrow.

"And also it goes back to that whistle. You didn't pray right when you got that thing fix."

The whistle lies unwrapped in the middle of the dining table. Gretta watches Angela circle around the kitchen about a dozen times, cleaning spots off the refrigerator, the counter, the cupboards. She stops in the middle, turns around, and inspects her work.

What would she want with my dictionary?

The light from the kitchen window is bright—too bright for such a dark little room. She sees sun spots. The air smells like rain, but if it rained last night, there is no visible trace of it now. The air is dry. Thick. Gretta can sense moisture being sucked out of each and every cell in her body, taking her oxygen. Someone will pay for her dictionary, and given the delicate situation she is in, it might as well not be Lance.

"Your friend who got the hantavirus—did you pray for her?" Gretta says. "Yeah? You did? Because she's *dead.* Maybe you don't pray right either."

Lance leans forward, as if preparing to leap between them.

Angela is undeterred. "You. You think that whistle would have broke otherwise? I'm not talking about my friend. I'm talking about you. You got to pray for your marriage, pray for your children."

That's when Gretta sees the fingers working the polka-dotted shoelaces, the tiny knuckles brushing against the maroon carpeting. Her own black boots next to them. *Are you logical, too, Mom?* Logic. She could use some logic now. Now that her dictionary is gone, the need is greater.

She can't ask her for it. She can't demand it back. But she can try to unseat her, even with the old woman's eyes steadfast and the air thick as it is. She pushes past: "Does God listen to some people's prayers and not to others? Because I really want to know." Gretta's voice cracks, shakes. She is flushed with humiliation.

Lance's head is in his hands. She sees his head in his mistress's lap. Her anger usurps her will to bring him home. She wants him to look up, to look at her. To gauge something—she doesn't know what.

"If you prayed, you would know," says Angela.

"Or does God listen sometimes, but not all the time? Doesn't God like it here on the reservation? And what's up with the mice? Why does he send mice to fuck with you people? For us it was rats. I guess we didn't pray right either."

It's as if her mouth has a conviction of its own. She feels like an idiot for being inarticulate, guilty for spouting off about nothing, desperate for her loss.

"I was sick and I got better," says Angela. "I prayed. Lance was sick with alcohol and he got better. We all prayed for him and he prayed with us. Look at you—the police bring you to my house drunk and maybe that drug too. You should be with your kids." Her eyes water and her voice rises and falls in pieces.

Gretta tries to let the fury go, but she can't. *There shall be no smiting here.* She wants a change, at least. She wants something to take her out.

But she wants first to get to the bottom of this praying business. She is worried Angela might be right; she wants badly to prove her wrong.

"Did your grandson's heart fail because his parents prayed Catholic?"

"They believe in that cross," Lance mumbles. "I don't like that cross."

"So that's why he died. Because they use crosses and God doesn't like crosses. He likes medicine wheels. He likes symmetry." Four arms, four legs, all brown. *Does he give her oral sex? Does he tell her about you? "You should meet my wife."*

"See, Lance on the other hand, he likes three-ways."

"I'm not talking about God," yells Lance. "If you would listen sometimes, you might hear something. All this might not have happened."

"I heard something." Gretta tries to regain her composure. *Sheep. Lots and lots of sheep.*

"The Creator," Angela says, nodding her head. "The Creator wants you to admit that thing."

"I heard you have a girlfriend." *Inhale two, three…exhale….*

Lance doesn't respond. His silence rests in her throat. Angela is still talking, but Gretta doesn't hear her. Finally, Lance looks up at her. He stares hard as if she might reveal a bluff.

"Yeah? I heard something too." His voice lowers, and she feels it in her fingertips. "Dear James."

She begins to shake. *Inhale two, three…exhale two, three, four….*

Angela's son-in-law Randal walks into the kitchen and puts his hands on the edge of the table. "It ain't God's fault. It's because sometimes the people around them are so strong and so bad, God can't do anything to help," he says. He tosses the dictionary on the table. "This yours?"

Lance smirks at her. She doesn't care. She has it back. With that, she can walk out of the room. She can go home. She can eat lunch. She can have sex with whomever she pleases. She can even throw the book away.

"What're you talking about?" Angela says to Randal. "You don't know what you're talking about. You sit home all day and all night. You should be out there working. You need to pray too." She chastises him in Navajo again.

"And Lance! If you knew your own language you would know what I said. You got to learn. That's who you are and who you are supposed to be. You just forget about it. That's why things don't work out for you."

She turns to Gretta. "And you. You admit that thing right now!"

Gretta tries to look squarely at Lance and comes close to it. *Admit to what? Admit to which?* Jeff? Alcoholism? Getting fired? Maybe they all had read her files—gathered round, ate popcorn: *I fucked around before the tequila man ever existed.* Why doesn't Angela ask *Lance* to "admit that thing"? He's as guilty as she is; she's sure of it. Probably more. *What does he do when he leaves? Who does he see? Who does he touch? How many?* She wants to say it, but she doesn't know how much Angela knows. She doesn't want her involved any more than she already is—in anything. *And who is to touch me?*

Who has touched me? How many? How bad was it?

"They had a ceremony at my mom and dad's last week," Lance says. "Erikson found something with hair in it behind a brick in the old house."

"You came through Salt Lake and didn't stop?"

"You got to pray for yourself. You tell the truth, and you pray, and things might get better," says Angela.

"Are you saying you came through Salt Lake and didn't stop to see your kids? Your wife?"

"Someone wrapped hair and a scrap of my shirt in it and put the brick back over it."

"Yeah? So?"

"They think you did it."

"Oh, for Christ's sake. They do not."

"It doesn't matter!"

"What do you mean, it doesn't matter? They think I *witched* you?

What is this, the seventeenth fucking century? Burn me at the stake, then."

"It's not the same—" He takes a deep breath and blows out impatience, frustration. Gretta knows this sign—he's about to lose it. Strangely, he doesn't. "Look, I know you didn't do it."

"As if I would know how—"

"I *said* it doesn't matter."

"Did you see it? Did you see the little bag and the hair and the—the shirt?"

"I said it doesn't matter."

"Did you or didn't you?"

"No...I didn't go outside."

"And the whistle," says Randal. "Don't forget what he said about that whistle."

"What about the whistle?"

"Erikson didn't say that!" Lance says. "She said it." He nods toward Angela. And to Gretta: "You broke that too, she said. She said it broke because of you. We weren't right together. That's what she said."

"Jesus. She and your mother both...."

"Well, it kind of did. I mean, not because of you. I'm not saying...but in my back pocket, when I got in the car that day we left for Salt Lake."

"Yeah, yeah, heard it. Many times. For a *decade.* Thank you, Renee."

"You pray, and you tell the truth. You got your chance right now," says Angela.

"Pray for *what?*" She coats it in sarcasm, but she asks herself whether it really is a rhetorical question.

"Pray for yourself, for your family, to live in a good way. To give up that drink and all those bad things it is you do."

Gretta holds her head, which has been shaking side to side, side to side. *Side to side, side to side.*

"Mom! I know you're just worried about me, but you're going to have to back off. She's my wife. You get it? Just leave her alone. *Please.*"

Mom. The hair on Gretta's arms stands on end. "Aunt!" she wants to scream. "Aunt!" She reminds herself it's just a tradition. *Just a tradition?* And then it occurs to her that he has defended her—really defended her. The bumps on her skin remain, but now as a small elation.

Lance excuses himself to the restroom. Gretta nabs the dictionary. "It was laying outside there on the street," Randal says. "I figured it had to be yours."

"Thanks. Thank you."

Angela sits down at the table and cries silently, alternately sucking her lips in and pushing them out, her fingers fussing with a placemat. She prays quietly in Navajo, every syllable softened by tiny gusts and gasps of air.

Gretta gets herself a glass of water without asking—for practice, maybe. For fun. Just opens Angela's cupboard door and takes a glass. "What do you pray for, Randy?" Gretta asks, standing on top of the goose, trembling nonetheless.

"I don't know. I just pray to hell I get some money quick, or my wife'll kick me out." Lance returns to the kitchen to sit by his aunt. He and Randal laugh nervously. Angela begins lashing Randal with Navajo again and Gretta laughs too, in spite of herself. She laughs that Angela's tongue is so dexterous, her voice itself reaching an impenetrable beauty. Laughs that everyone else seems to be ignoring the old woman now. Laughs that her children might never forgive her. That Lance has become involved with someone else. The laugh sounds strange in her ear and she forces herself to stop.

She feels woozy. She wipes her nose, her eyes. "Lance," *honk,* "could you get me some Benadryl, please? I need some sleep before I drive." *Honk honk.*

"Call your mom first. Tell her we'll be home tomorrow," he says.

They'll Eat My Irises

"Ruthless: Having no ruth: MERCILESS, CRUEL." Gretta reads aloud from *WordsforLater*. Her voice is mostly lost over the wind crossing through the windows, so she strains to read louder.

"*Rutilant: To glow reddish: having a reddish glow.* That one's nice, isn't it? No?" She had the small victory of being defended for a good couple of hours before images of the rumored lovebirds started whittling away at her again.

"Ruttish: Inclined to rut: LUSTFUL. Rutty: Full of ruts."

"Please stop," says Lance.

She opens *Dispatches* to a page she had dogeared. "Page forty-nine, wouldn't you know? 'Straight history, auto-revised history, history without handles, for all the books and articles and white papers…something wasn't answered, it wasn't even asked. We were backgrounded, deep, but when the background started sliding forward—'"

"Gretta, please…."

She tries to read his level of irritation.

"Why did you cut your hair?" she asks. He doesn't answer. "Someone die?" She waits again, cocks her head dramatically, until it occurs to her that someone may have, in fact, died. *James? Grandma Shiprock?* But it wasn't his dad's side that cut their hair to mourn. It was his mother's side. *James?*

"I wondered when you'd notice," he says, stroking his neck, which has been squared off by razor. "I guess I didn't need it anymore." He smiles at her. "Don't worry, no one died."

She puts the book away and closes the laptop. She sets the computer on the floor and pretends to study her hands. When the truck slows, Gretta looks up.

"Flea market?" she asks. Lance nods. He climbs out of the pickup. She follows.

Her hands soon become filmy, fingering shrunken clothes and unobtainable, heavy silver-and-turquoise jewelry. She used to think she'd have a squash necklace one day, or at least a bracelet. She thought eventually they'd have plenty of money and Lance would prettify and legitimize her with turquoise.

"I can't believe you're just going to leave the car here with your aunt," she says.

"She needs it. We can get by with the truck."

"What will you drive when we get home?"

"I'll take the bus. For a while."

"You won't take the bus."

"Gretta, please—we'll figure something out. That thing couldn't be worth more than eight hundred dollars. Is it such a big deal?"

"Yeah, it's a big deal. We can't just buy another one for eight hundred dollars—not one that works. Our credit sucks. I lost my job. Did I tell you that?"

"Don't say that—please don't."

She glares at him, at his response.

"Shit. Gretta—"

"You up and quit your job," she says. "You didn't think twice about it."

"And I got another one."

"Where?"

"It's not important."

"Where?"

"Refinery."

"In Farmington?"

He nods.

"That's just great. Hydrochloric acid? Xylene? Benzene?"

"At least I have a job. And you're so full of liquor…don't tell me about contamination."

"What are we doing here, anyway? All I want is a cigarette. Why can't I find a cigarette in this furnace? Let's go to a *store* store."

He pulls a cigarette out of his jacket pocket. "It's not that hot."

"You've been holding out on me?" says Gretta.

"Do you want it or not?"

She lights up the cigarette in front of an old woman's stand. The gesture is not appreciated. *To hell with her bun*. She breathes in deep, deep as she can, and stifles a cough.

"I've got to get back to the kids. You have to decide what you want, Lance."

"What I want? Why is it what I want? We're leaving right after this—going home."

"You're the one who's been living with someone else." She tries to stop herself, to dam up the bitchiness that seems to flood her, but she can't. She can't stop wishing for a drink. And she certainly can't say *that* out loud, not now.

"I haven't been living with her. I've been living with Angela and Jerry."

"So you agree it's a her? It's a specific person—I say *her* and you know who I'm talking about?"

"Come on—you've been hinting around about her all morning. Don't act like you don't know. I want to know what *you* want."

Yes, she knew. Sort of. She'd suspected. She'd been told. But being almost certain is not the same as hearing it out of his mouth; the affection with which he says *her* alone is too much to stomach.

"What I want? I want to be normal." A sound issues from her throat—not a sob, but a gurgle. *Don't cry.* "I want to have a normal family with a husband who's not fucking someone else."

"I'm not fucking her. She's having sex. Just not with me. Not now."

"Right. Right." Gretta is not sure what to be concerned about now. She's confused. She knows he's hiding something, but his lies are usually simple. She decides it's a complexity she doesn't want to unravel. "We're never going to be normal, you and me."

"What's normal?" he says.

"We're never going to be happy."

"So let's get a divorce," he says—maybe with sarcasm, maybe not.

"Yeah." It's what she wants, sometimes. It's what seems bound to happen—a nontraditional turn toward tradition, maybe.

"Wait here," he says. "I have to go talk to someone." He walks off, disappearing between a couple of vans.

Gretta is losing track of what tradition means. It used to mean something like putting the same ornaments on the Christmas tree year after year. Or it meant something bad—like conservatism or misogyny. Then she met Lance and the word gained momentum, became something fat and inaccessible. His family quickly learned she had no concept of tradition. She was careless and uncooperative. She walked around the north side of the sweat lodge when she entered. She coughed on the Indian tobacco. She doused her fry bread in butter, then sprinkled it with sugar and cinnamon. She was, nevertheless, expected to take part *in the tradition*.

In keeping with tradition, Lance and Gretta were married the Navajo way. Everything was supposed to be exactly right for the wedding—the turquoise, the basket, the corn. Lance's parents had talked about giving horses to Gretta's parents since his mother could get them free from Wyoming. "And put them in my backyard?" her mother said. "They'll eat my irises. I just planted shrubs." Gretta told her they were kidding and not to worry—it would never happen. And it didn't.

There was supposed to be a gift or a payment of sorts from the groom's parents to the bride's. Maybe the horses were a joke, but the idea she knew to be true. She wasn't happy about being bought, but she was more unhappy to find out she wasn't being bought. "Everything must go just the way it is, the tradition," Lance's father had said when they first planned the wedding. "Otherwords, it's not right." So it's possible that the tradition meant nothing, in which case they had spent more than six hundred dollars on a tipi—being possibly hundreds of miles away from the closest hogan—not to mention the feast that would have fed a staff of zookeepers, the expensive basket it took them months to find, the velvet and the mock-satin that proved nearly impossible to sew into wedding outfits, the payment to the medicine man—all this, all for show.

Gretta supposes that doesn't make it different from any other wedding, with white gowns and flowers and altars and such. The only thing that means anything is the contract, the marriage license. And that only matters in the case of health insurance. Or divorce, when you pay to have the license revoked. *Jesus,* she thinks, *there must be something else to getting wedded.*

But that isn't what bothers her most. The more painful possibility is that his parents intentionally tripped on the wedding tradition because they didn't want the marriage to work out. She wonders if they succeeded.

"Is getting a divorce traditional if you remarry an Indian?" she asks Lance when he reappears behind her, one hand on her shoulder, another hand holding twin ShopKo bags full of stuff.

"What kind of a question is that?" He acts so nonchalant it hurts her. He flicks his cigarette on the pavement and inspects a knife.

She wonders how visitation works these days. One weekend every couple of weeks? She could live with the kids being gone four days out of the month. It might be the kids' only chance at seeing him regularly. Would he show up? *He hasn't so far.*

"Come on, we can't stay here all day," says Lance.

"Oh, please. I'm waiting for you."

"Waiting for me to what?"

"Get the keys. Get the truck. What are we doing here?" *This is not what I want.* The thought is thunderous in her head. "Whatever. You go get the car, please. Please."

The idea is to get by from one moment to the next. To hope that something good will happen. There's not much else she can do except give up and die, and she can't do that. She has kids to take care of. She has an addiction to overcome. She has tickets to the Chinese acrobats that she won on the radio. Anyway, suicide didn't work out when she was fifteen, nineteen, twenty-three, twenty-six, or locked in the motel room with the fox, so it probably wouldn't happen now.

This is not what I want. This is not what I want. She has exhausted her options. *What you need is a serious accident.*

She is ushered to her banged-up chariot. The ease with which she takes the passenger seat scares her. "If you want to be with an Indian man, you're going to have to learn to walk behind him," Sylvia told her one day when she showed up at Gretta's door. Lance had sent her to say something in his defense after an argument, thinking his sister could, perhaps, patch things up between them. "Say you wake up and make him pancakes and he decides he wants eggs and bacon and oatmeal. What do you do? You give the pancakes to the dogs and start all over." Gretta wishes Lance could have heard his sister then, so he could understand why she could never, ever cook him eggs and bacon and oatmeal. Sylvia is different now that she's out of college—more independent, less likely to cook eggs and bacon and oatmeal all at the same time. But maybe she isn't so different. Maybe then she was just saying the very thing she knew Gretta wouldn't want to hear so "the little white girl" would leave her brother alone—red tape, just like the wedding gift to her parents that never arrived. She wonders why Sylvia's disdain wasn't as obvious to Lance—why he would trust his sister to mediate.

To Lance's credit, he never asked his wife to be his cook. If she made him pancakes, he said thanks and, more often than not, did the dishes afterward.

When he starts the pickup, Gretta opens his sacks. Pink pajamas, six to nine months. More pink pajamas. More pink pajamas. A daisy-print shirt, denim overalls, yellow booties. Three pacifiers. Four bottles. A large can of Similac. A tiny silver bracelet with a turquoise center, just like the one he gave Tulip when she was a baby. A note—

He turns the ignition off. "Please don't," he says. He underscores his words with an uncharacteristically steady stare. She folds the note up slowly and puts it back in the sack, which she tucks beside her feet. "I'm trying, Gretta. I'm trying very hard. I love you, and I love our kids, and I'm going to keep trying. Are you trying?"

Am I? Devoid of an answer, she says she is sorry. He starts the truck up again, gives her a cigarette. She smiles, to the extent that she can.

Or What

LANCE WALKS briskly from the store to the pickup, his hands prone as if to hold footballs, and gets in. "They said you already had your prescription sent to Moab. And to Monticello. And to Cortez."

Gretta tries to gather her thoughts. She remembers calling and sitting in the parking lot in Moab—*Para Español, marqué uno*—maybe calling Monticello, but she didn't pick anything up.

"Did you hear me? First you had a refill sent to Moab, then you had it sent to Monticello, then you called from Cortez—"

You couldn't have made it to Cortez, could you have? "I know one thing, I didn't pick anything up. Or I'd have it."

"You have kids, Gretta. You can't do this again."

"What?"

"You know what. Why are you trying to get three months' worth of Dilantin?"

"I'm trying to get one month—just my prescription. I'm out. Totally. I ran out last week—"

"Last week?" he shouts.

She is so nervous, she can't seem to talk. There is so much time she can't account for. So much has been left unexplained. What does she know? The ambiguity presses, it pushes, it forces itself on her, and she just sits there, wishing for the moment to be over. "I mean, maybe not a whole week."

"Christ, Gretta, you can't just go off it like that." He chews his bottom lip; his eyes dart. He doesn't sound really angry; maybe he's just thinking. "Are you saying you didn't pick anything up from Moab?"

"No."

"Or anything from Monticello? Or Cortez?"

She's pretty sure she didn't so much as walk into a store in Monticello, except to fill up at the gas station. And Cortez—nothing comes to mind. Of course, that's nothing new. She could check her pack, her receipts, her phone, but she doesn't want to call attention to her craziness.

"No."

"What about the LSD?"

"What LSD?"

"They found a hit of acid in the pickup. You're damned lucky.... Fuck. Are you going to do it again, or what?"

"Do what?"

"You *know* what I'm talking about."

Depends on whether you're coming home, she thinks, but feels guilty even thinking of it. She would never blackmail him with suicide. Not intentionally. There's a lot she would do—drop a naked guy off at the side of the road, for instance; maybe even give James the green light, finally—but she wouldn't try to make someone feel responsible for her suicide.

"I promise I won't."

"Because you can't leave Tulip and Braden behind. If you're going to pull something like that, you need to tell me. Seriously. It's not fair to them."

"*You* left them behind."

"It's not that I left them *behind.* I've been...rearranging. I've been trying to sort everything out, make a plan, save money. I never intended to leave them and not come back."

"Come back, or come back for them?"

"I don't know."

"You don't know? Whether you planned to take my children away from me?"

"I mean, one minute you're in the hospital, the next minute you're being hauled off by cops...what am I supposed to do?"

"That was one time. One time I went to the hospital…it was the seizures. You heard the neurologist."

"I heard him say psychosis was *rare.*"

"And only one time have I gone to jail."

"Not including last night—"

"They didn't charge me with anything, did they? They took me to Angela's."

"They could have. You could've got a DUI, possession, resisting arrest—"

"I'm *there* for them. I read to them. I take them to the zoo, to the children's museum, to the planetarium. I take Tulip to school, Braden to daycare, we do flashcards together…I go grocery shopping. Do you go grocery shopping?" Gretta has a hard time holding his stare, even though it's fast becoming less resentful and more conciliatory. "Braden knows his colors. You didn't know that, did you? And who are you? Three DUIs."

Lance starts up the pickup again. "That was a long time ago. I changed."

"I'll change."

"You always say you'll change."

He has her: she always says she'll change.

You'll change? Okay, who has the upper hand, here? Let's think. Who takes off on a dime?

"You'll get into a program?"

"What, like rehab?"

"Fuck." He turns the pickup off again and rests against the steering wheel.

Good thing the starter's fixed, she thinks. And, *Should I rub it in? No man to fix my vehicle, no way*. And, *Why should you have to tell him anything?*

He seems to be crying, or maybe he's shaking from laughter, she can't tell for certain. She doesn't have a job—she can't even pay for daycare in order to work at twelve cents a word—so she has the time for rehab, but not the money. Can the state really turn her away? She'd looked into it before; no real welcome mat presented itself, which seemed to be a sign that she didn't need it. Maybe Lance's plan is to get her into rehab then spirit her kids away from her. They could be raised by the woman with the baby, by Lance's girlfriend. *Do you have to use that word?* And, *You could just consider it a chance to get straight.* But why couldn't she just stop? Let sobriety *transpire*? She's cut way down for the Dilantin, until the past couple of weeks. Surely she could cut herself off. *Can't I?* She realizes the trip was indeed a very bad idea. If she had totally dried out instead of become saturated right before her little adventure…but then she never would have made it out of Salt Lake City. She would have waited for a call. And waited. And waited. Just as she had been waiting for months.

"And while we're on it, what about the shovel?"

"The shovel?"

"No. Stop. I don't even want to know."

"What shovel?"

"The bloody shovel they found in the pickup! The blood on the seat, on the seatbelt. You know, they kept the shovel. Just in case. It was a big fucking favor to me they even brought you home. What have you gotten yourself into? Never mind. I don't even want to know."

"A fox. I hit it. I put it in the car—I strapped it in. The shovel…I had to scrape him off, you know. The fox…it's at a hotel."

"You strapped a dying fox into our pickup? Is this like the magpie that took your wedding ring? The snow boy that wandered into the driveway? The Russian indigent that lit the shed on fire? The wind storm—"

"Oh, forget it. You don't want to know, right? You don't even want to know." Theirs, she realizes, will be a long drive home—longer, in some respects, than the drive to get here.

The Image Lasts All the Way Across

SHE WAKES UP to Lance pulling off on an exit and into a small town. She thinks he's going to stop for fast food, but he passes McDonald's, KFC, Four Corners Burgers and Shakes. He keeps driving—turning off in the wrong direction: south.

"Where are we going?" she asks Lance.

"Get some sleep."

They drive along barren roads until curiosity turns to anxiety and then to panic. But (*questions, questions*) she is afraid to ask why they have come this way. Finally he pulls onto a dirt road and parks next to a wood-shingled white house.

He looks at her for some time. "I'm going to ask you this once," he says. The tone is not good. Her heart knows it and beats indiscriminately. He looks as afraid as she feels. He waits. For what, she doesn't understand. Then: "Did you fuck him?"

"Who?"

"What do you mean, who? My brother."

Oh, him. Thank you. Because she can honestly say no.

"Of course not."

"No? Or not that you can remember?"

"No. Absolutely not." That, she would remember.

He breathes in the manner of Olympic divers just before jetting off to the end of the high dive. He stares at the porch a moment. He grabs the two white sacks. "Wait here."

He slings the sacks over his shoulder and knocks. A woman answers the door. She's slender and pretty. Her black hair turns in just below the shoulders. Lance disappears inside the house. She is no relative of Lance; she must be the one, the girlfriend. Gretta's skin burns cold, hot, cold, hot.

You could go in—

She reaches up, up from the tarry pit, but she can only find two radio stations—country and evangelical babble.

She pushes her swollen feet into sandals and gets out. An Austrailian shepherd mix runs up to her, barking, baring his teeth. She jumps back into the cab. "Lance!" The dog is noisy and snotty but not particularly foamy. Lance appears on the porch with the woman, who calls the dog off. The dog runs behind the house.

"Fucking lush! Stupid drunk!" she yells at Gretta. And at Lance: "You deserve her!" She pushes him—"Asshole!"—and slams the door.

Lance stands near the porch a minute, staring at the shut door.

He knocks. "I need my tape recorder!" The door opens. The tape recorder flies halfway to the truck and busts into black pieces and a tape.

Give him the whistle. The whistle—why is it still in two pieces? Erikson said he'd fix it, he'd drill holes on both ends, then Lance would have two. He gave him a smaller female whistle for the meantime, the meantime turning into years, when he gave the two pieces back—with no new holes drilled on both ends. The new whistle, it still had meat on it, like a wishbone the week after Thanksgiving. Lance never used the female. He said the children's plumes were enough to protect them. *Protect them*—are they protected? *Your mother is protecting your children. Good god.*

Lance waits on the little white porch. She wants to call him to her. She wants to beat him with a sharp stick. *Just give him the whistle.*

The woman comes out of the house crying. She sits on the porch, her head tucked under her arms. Lance sits by her, puts an arm around her. He pets her back. She lifts her head up. Her puffy face is blackened by makeup. He wipes her face with his hand and presses her head against his shoulder. "Shh," he says. "It's all right." For a second

Gretta feels as though it could be her he's consoling, but the comfort comes as a drop of water on the dry, dry earth.

The dog pokes its head from behind the house and barks. A baby cries. Gretta wants to see for herself but waits, hoping her face is not as red as it feels. She tosses around the clothes and dirty napkins and fast-food bags that are strewn all over the cab. It occurs to her she can check out the dates accessed on her files to figure out what Lance has seen and what he has not. Then she concurs with herself that, at this point, it doesn't matter anyway.

The yard has no grass. There is a cactus at the side of the house. It sends up hot pink. She hears her pulse and takes notice of her breath—short, sharp, shocked. She breathes in deeply and exhales slowly. *Pneumatic.*

"Aren't you afraid—what if something happens to your whistle?" she asked Lance when they left it with Erikson at his trailer house so long ago.

"Like what?" he asked.

"What if he forgets it's yours? What if someone takes it from him?"

"Why would anyone take it? It hasn't been given to them."

Vacuous.

An old Pinto is pulled half apart thirty yards back. It was brown then green…or green then brown. Now it's rusted, just like her own truck. She scoots to the driver's side of the cab. She forgets the starter is fixed, so when the ignition turns over smooth as wet soap, it is as a gift rather than the consequence of a mechanic.

"What kind of Indian am I?" Tulip asked her one day.

"You're two kinds—Cheyenne on Grandma's side and Navajo on Grandpa's," she answered.

"What kind are you?" she asked again.

"I'm English, Dutch…Welsh?—and maybe a lot of other stuff."

"So what kind am I?" she asked.

Lance calls after her, but the truck is in motion. He yells louder. The situation is beyond her. There's nothing she can do except go forward, anywhere. *Isn't it what you wanted? What you wanted all along?*

His skin was soft and spongy. She thought she could never do without it. Maybe she can.

She wants to curse his mother, his aunt, his lover. But it's not about them. It's about her—and also about him, and there's no undoing any of it. She reaches under the seat for her bottle, stuffs it between her legs, and uncaps. She drinks long, with gratitude, because with any luck, with any waft of transpiration, tonight will be the night before she'll show back up at her caseworker's door, asking for help. "It was an Occident," she'll tell her. "It was purely Occidental." And whatever the woman tells her to do, short of giving up her children, she'll do.

She wonders about the crying baby. What does she look like? Does she look like Lance? They almost took in a little girl a couple of years ago—her teenaged cousin's baby. Lance didn't think it was a good idea. It wasn't good for the children, he said. She figured Lance didn't want any more kids. By the looks of things, he doesn't. But maybe he wants her—the woman on the porch. *Maybe you want a woman.* Maybe she wants a lot of things.

She thinks about the baby and insurance and government housing and those Twelve fucking Steps, the ones she gets stuck on, and together they make a black hole. The baby isn't aware of any of this, of life in general, even. It's all mom, milk, my diaper's wet. One day she might have to introduce Tulip and Braden to a sister. They might be photographed together, and the photograph could very well be suspended on her fridge with an I ♥ Arizona magnet. The future—it could be anything. She tries to imagine that, but instead she sees just a shell of a baby, because for now, she isn't prepared to see anything else. There are some places she will have to go alone, but there is one place she'd far rather be: with her kids. All she wants now, at this moment, is to look at them, to sleep between them, listen to them breathe; she wants to make sure that they haven't become a part of the emptiness. She wants to feel the fullness of their company, because that is as close to God as she is willing and able to get. It is her red road, her white road, her only road.

Lance will surely show up someday. Maybe she will be dry, and he will ask to stay. Maybe she'll say no. Maybe she and the kids will run off with James—or Bincy, for that matter, or just with themselves—somewhere far away. Or maybe she'll say, "Of course" and "I love you," and everything will be different, as it was for Renee and Clyde when they gave up drinking for singing. But she can't bring him or anyone else home this way. Not like this—not couched in a living, breathing, drunken apology. And not in the face of a brown-eyed, beautiful emissary to a world that would have her drown from a mountaintop—not with this woman, who will be, in Gretta's mind, forever waiting in her driveway, holding a baby that is or is not Lance's. *Not like this.*

The future, it could be anything. She moves, the whole of her: forward, home.

Afterword: Gretta's Alternative Twelve Steps to Sobriety

1. I conceded that I had long entertained the power of alcohol to console myself of the fact that life is by nature unmanageable.

2. Came to believe that this power of alcohol was not enough to restore me to sanity, or, alternatively, to suspend my concern about my sanity, or my doubt in that rhetorical category, sanity.

3. Made a decision to turn my will into knowledge as I felt compelled to pursue it, since I understood that I understand little and have an insatiable need to understand all.

4. Made a searching (if fearful and incomplete) inventory of questions about who and what the fuck my "self" might be.

5. Admitted in a drunken stupor at the company Christmas party the inexact nature of my many shortfallings, including a short holiday fall off the wagon. Hopped back on the next day; apologized for telling a coworker his tie was too short.

6. Was entirely unconvinced that a deity—if one existed—could or would be interested in removing any of my defects of character. Decided I didn't need convincing.

7. Humbly admitted I would have to remedy some or all of my defects my own damned self, and quick.

8. Made a list of all of the times I had put myself and my kids at risk and admitted to my shrink that I could have opted not to.

9. Amends: to put right; *especially*: to make emendations in (as a text); to change or modify for the better: IMPROVE <*amend*

the situation>; to alter, *especially*: to alter formally by modification, deletion, or addition <*amend* a constitution>; *intransitive verb*: to reform oneself.

10. Continued to warehouse an inventory of mostly irrelevant questions about the self, and when I deluded myself into answers, promptly admitted I was, in fact, delusional.

11. Sought through pottery classes and picnics and even dreaded *play dates* to remain willfully conscious despite an urge to step in front of a truck.

12. Having posted these steps on my bedroom mirror, I was able to get through the day. And the day after that. And the day after that. And so on.

And I will get through the day—until I don't.

Acknowledgments

LOVE AND gratitude to my husband David and daughters Brigitte and Kate and to my parents and siblings for their encouragement and patience, to my sister Michele Allen for reading my book, and to my fiction-writing teachers, Karen Brennan, Dori Sanders, Rikki Ducornet, Terese Svoboda, Steve Almond, David Foster Wallace, and most especially Francois Camoin, for making me feel free, if only in theory. Love and thanks also to Tomo Hattori, E. Ethelbert Miller, Darrell Spencer, Shelley Hunt, Terryn Berry, Roger Wallins, D'Wayne Hodgin, and Ed Hughes. I am especially indebted to my editor John Alley, to Guy Lebeda and Liz Smith at the Utah Arts Council, and to those who helped me grapple with this manuscript, Annette Ephroni, John Pecorelli, and Brian Kubarcyz, and to John McCallum for cover art.